Take A Shot

Van Cole

Published by Van Cole, 2023.

This is a work of fiction. Similarities to real people, places, or events are entirely coincidental.

TAKE A SHOT

First edition. January 9, 2023.

Copyright © 2023 Van Cole.

ISBN: 979-8223054016

Written by Van Cole.

Table of Contents

Chapter 1...1
Chapter 2...5
Chapter 3...10
Chapter 4...14
Chapter 5...18
Chapter 6...22
Chapter 7...27
Chapter 8...30
Chapter 9...35
Chapter 10...38
Chapter 11...41
Chapter 12...46
Chapter 13...51
Chapter 14...55
Chapter 15...59
Chapter 16...67
Chapter 17...74
Chapter 18...78
Chapter 19...82
Chapter 20...87
Chapter 21...91
Epilogue..98

Take A Shot

MM First Time Hockey Romance

By: Van Cole

Foreword

Dan is a professional hockey player at the top of his game – but when his wife up and leaves him out of nowhere, it feels like game, set and match. How is he supposed to get through his upcoming games with an apartment empty of furniture, and his wife off sleeping with some baseball player she's supposedly been seeing for a while now?

Turns out, however, that Dan's life isn't finished loading things onto him yet. When Dan's college flame Jeremy walks back onto the scene, after years of Dan convincing himself that he's *not* gay, and that his father was right about everything? Well, it completely screws his head up. The ghost of something special and more intimate is definitely hanging around him, but he thought his days of wanting men were long behind him.

No question about it, Dan's life is a mess – but maybe if he follows his instincts, they'll take him where he needs to go. After all, they've never failed him in a hockey game. They should know what to do. Right?

The only problem is, Jeremy isn't the only obstacle walking around Dan's life right now – and at least Jeremy is harmless. Dan's wife may have unceremoniously left him, but she's definitely not done screwing with him yet...

Take A Shot

Chapter 1

"There is something seriously wrong with you. I don't know what it is, but there is."

"Something wrong with me?"

Sarah looked at him like he was an alien, clearly unimpressed with this response. Her long brown curls dangled down her back, bouncing with her head as she talked. Dan thought she looked somewhat childish when she did that. Sometimes he really couldn't stand her and didn't know why he had married her to begin with – but he guessed that most marriages included bugbears like that. Spending so much time with just one person would highlight things you couldn't stand.

Right?

Back when they'd gotten together, Sarah had been a beacon of confidence, ambition, and warmth. Her wicked smile and dagger-sharp honesty had always endeared her to him, and he had valued the notion that she'd never lie to him. She'd never pretend to be happy when she wasn't, and she'd never let him get away with slacking off on his dreams. They had clicked, and it had been so good.

So when had all those things gone so bad? These days, he often couldn't stand the way she pressed him. He worked hard on the pitch and off it for his training. He didn't leave all the housework to her. The fact that she didn't seem to think he deserved some relaxation time set him on edge constantly – and her truths no longer seemed like constructive criticism so much as manipulative insults. Had she always been this way? He didn't know, but he could only hope it was a storm that was due to pass soon. He didn't know how much longer he could take it.

That being said, maybe he wouldn't have to.

"I just can't be with someone that doesn't seem to be present with me. You're always staring off into space like you'd rather be elsewhere, even during sex, Dan."

"That's not true."

"You think I don't notice?" she bit back, and his white lie died in his mouth. Okay, he had been getting distracted in bed recently – but he hadn't wanted to hurt her feelings by agreeing. "I don't know if there's another woman, or if it's the game, but I'm done, Dan. Find someone else to play your stupid mind games with."

Dan just stood there, confused. Running his hand through his unruly black hair, he could only stare at her. He never understood what she meant when she talked like that – rather, he knew exactly what she was saying, but he had no idea why she would say it. Of course, there was no other woman, and it was off-season in hockey right now.

"Sarah, what are you talking about? I am with you. I'm right here. I am always right here. Sure, I've been a little tired lately; we're coming up to the friendly with the Penguins next week, and it's hard training, but... I didn't think things had gotten this bad. Please explain to me what I am missing?"

She stood there a moment, staring at him. He could almost see in her eyes that she was trying to figure out why she had married him. She had obviously loved him at one point – used to tell him that he was gorgeous, every woman's dream. Muscular, handsome face, cocky and sweet at the same time, what was not to love? But by the look he was seeing from her now, she could no longer stand the sight of him. Too much had happened in their short marriage that could not be fixed – especially if she was going to let this communication logjam build up until it all came out in this one, long tirade.

"Dan, I have tried too many times to explain anything to you. But it's like you don't hear me. You are always so far away; your mind is always elsewhere. I am tired of competing. I love you, but I am gone. I'm going to go stay with Devon for a while."

Now – the rest, Dan could have understood, but this?

Well. This was something else entirely.

"Devon Adams? The baseball player? Seriously?" Dan wasn't a violent person despite his sport, but he couldn't help but feel the beginnings of anger heat up in his chest now. He certainly wouldn't pretend he was blameless in this scenario, as clearly, they had both contributed to the stagnation of their relationship – but it was as she mentioned Devon that he finally clicked what was going on. "You're going to make this argument sound like I'm the only one who's done something wrong, yet you're the one going to go stay with another man. You know what, Sarah? Take your drama queen ass and go be with your lover. I would never stand in the way of your dreams. Hope you're happy. I hear he has a well-used hot-tub. Better watch you don't get something Ajax can't wash off."

It wasn't at all like Dan to speak to anybody like this, which ought to have been a testament to how angry she had made him. Even Sarah seemed surprised to hear it come out of his mouth. Her own mouth gaped open, for once not speaking; before he could go on, she turned around, picked up the bag she had been standing next to, and walked out the door.

Dan couldn't help it. He wanted to yell, but no sound would come out. Instead, he started throwing things around the house. A lamp bounced off the wall and shattered as it hit the floor; the cushions from the couch landed in the dining area, where they narrowly missed knocking some shitty modern art sculpture down (her choice.) The coffee table ended up upside down 20 feet from where it started. Dan reached for the shelf lined with his hockey trophies but stopped himself before he overturned it. They, at least, did not deserve to be part of this mess.

He stood there in front of them, breath heavy. He hadn't much exerted himself. He was a professional hockey player, and his training put him through his paces way more than trashing a house in anger ever could – but the frustration rippled through his body like adrenaline. He couldn't even say he felt sad. It just seemed damn unfair.

Finally, his lips seemed to come unstuck. He cleared his throat. "This is not worth it. Damn stupid bullshit. You know what? Good riddance. Stupid shit got me talking to the walls now. What the hell?" He looked around the room at the disarray he'd caused, embarrassed despite the fact that nobody else was there to see it, and grunted in annoyance.

Dan went to the fridge and grabbed a beer. It was soon before the game, but fuck it; he felt the situation merited it. He chugged it before he'd even gotten more than a few feet from the fridge, so he grabbed another before heading into the living room.

It'd be a long night tonight. He was exhausted after the argument and the frustration, sure – but something told him he just wouldn't sleep well tonight. There were ghosts in his history that this marriage had chased away and now that she wasn't here – well. Who knew how long it would take them to resurface?

He scrubbed at his face, trying to focus on the shitty action movie that was playing in front of him, but he couldn't. He couldn't even focus on his feelings because he didn't know what to feel. Sarah had left. She'd said she was going for 'a while', but he doubted he could trust that. After all, she was going to stay with Devon. He was a mutual acquaintance, and too much of an asshole to be called a friend – but really, he had always known that Sarah could tolerate him way more than he himself could.

He just didn't know how much.

Chapter 2

A couple of days later, that game he'd been preparing for blew in. Dan's hockey team were good, and never went through the off-season without a few friendlies – but this time, the word 'friendly' was actually kind of a stretch. The game had been against a team with a pretty nasty reputation. One short week ago, he was bracing himself for a rough match.

Now, however, the roughness was exactly what he needed. He thought it would help him blow off some steam to play, beating up the other team's players – or at least defending his team when the other side beat up on them.

Unfortunately, however, it didn't. Even after they beat the crap out of them, he still felt drained. He'd thrown himself into training after Sarah had left, determined to distract himself rather than dwell on it, but of course, that hadn't been entirely effective. No man was an island and frustration was not a cure. As much as logic told him that the end of their marriage was for the better, he still couldn't help but feel a vague discomfort about losing something that was once good; he couldn't help but feel he'd failed in some way.

As a competitive man, he didn't take failure very well – and regardless of the fact that Sarah had contributed to that failure, he certainly couldn't say he enjoyed feeling it. Even winning the match couldn't cure that sense of loss.

After all, the match was only a friendly, played over the course of a couple of hours. His crumbled marriage was something he'd been trying to make work for years.

"Hey man, you going to sit there daydreaming all day? You should be partying, dude. We just won the finals and it is awesome!" Dan looked up at Zack, one of the newer members of their team. He had bright red hair that had a mind of its own and his face was covered in way too many freckles. But that seemed a turn-on for the ladies since he had a new girl almost every day. He was still a wild buck when it came to the game, but time would change that if he lasted.

Right now, Dan couldn't help but feel a little jealous of him – less for being a wild buck, and more for the women. It would probably do him good to play the field right now, but handsome as he was and as good as he'd probably be at it, promiscuity had never really been his scene. Even so, he couldn't let that jealousy show. It wasn't fair on Zack.

"Sorry, man, totally spaced out there."

Zack grinned at him, buying the story with ease. "Hey, I overheard Jason talking to Donovan about the captain throwing us a blow-out party if we won. Supposed to be at his place, but I'm not sure yet. You should come."

"Yeah, man, I'm just not feeling it right now. Maybe I'll stop by later, grab a couple of drinks or something."

"Yeah dude, all right. Maybe I'll see you there."

Dan looked back at his locker. He was confused. Was Zack hitting on him? He turned to look around at Zack who was at his locker pulling out his street clothes. Nah, he was probably just being friendly. His father had made sure he understood that gay guys didn't make it into pro sports back when he was in college. And besides, Zack was a ladies' man. But looking at Zack, he wondered, just, what if?

It was better to discard that kind of thought, though. No matter how many years it had been since his troubles, these things were better off left buried. Shaking his head, Dan grabbed the rest of his stuff, stood up from the bench and threw everything in his locker. Slamming it shut, he turned around and headed towards the door – but not before another of his teammates could stop him.

"Hey man, you coming to the party? It's going to be a blast! You should come." Dan looked around at Jason, who was grinning from ear to ear. Not that Jason ever smiled at him or anything – after all, they were quite a close-knit team – but something felt weird about this. He noticed almost everyone in the locker room was looking at him with a strange expression. Had they had already heard about Sarah and her bullshit with Devon? He couldn't see how they could possibly know about their breakup, as he and Sarah had been the only ones there, but he acknowledged there was a chance that her infidelity wasn't exactly a secret. Great! That was just what he needed right now, fake sympathy. He wondered how long it had been going on and how many of these asses had known and never told him.

Maybe some of them had even been with her behind his back.

Surely not, though. He liked to think he'd never done anything to any of these guys, and team morale was pretty good between them. As much as they tortured and teased each other, they were like brothers. They had to be in order to be successful.

These thoughts were useless, though. They were just distracting him from giving Jason an answer – and the very last thing he needed was for people to think he was losing his mind, not able to talk back to even basic questions.

"We'll see, maybe. Sounds like fun."

Jason shrugged. "I guess we'll see you if we see you, then."

When Dan got home, the place was bare. Sarah has come back while he was gone and took everything she wanted, including the television. That shit was pretty heavy, so maybe she'd brought Devon in to help her clear out. The thought of that made him feel pretty sick. He looks around and decides it not worth calling the cops, probably would be pointless anyway. They were legally married, after all, and it would only cause a stir in the media. He could imagine the headlines now, and they weren't exactly something he wanted to deal with – though knowing Sarah, she might end up speaking to the press anyway.

At any rate, she had left his clothes, the bed, and the couch, so at least he had some things left to live with. He walked into the kitchen to grab something to eat right quick – but opening the refrigerator, he realizes that, as her final 'screw you', she had taken all of the food and the dishes. Of course, she had. He suddenly remembered a time a few months back when she had insisted they go and buy new designer kitchenware, and the hours of painful shopping they'd spent as she chose exactly the right ones. He, of course, had footed the bill.

All for nothing.

Frustrated, Dan decides he would rather not spend the night alone and goes upstairs to shower. He wasn't in the mood to party, but he certainly wasn't in the mood to spend a night in this place, either – especially without even a TV to entertain and distract him.

After putting on clean clothes, Dan heads out to the party. Not sure whether it's at the captain's house or elsewhere, he starts making phone calls to get a ride. He finally gets ahold of Zack who is glad to pick him up.

"Hey, man. You're coming after all?"

"Seems that way."

"That's good," said Zack. There was something almost protective in his tone of voice. There was the brotherly bond after all. "Seems like you were a little off today, maybe that'll do you some good."

"I guess we'll see."

When Zack shows up, Dan is already outside waiting. The fresh air on the street was better than the empty apartment. With so little furniture in there, every footstep seemed to echo off the walls and bounce back and forth around him. It wasn't that he wanted Sarah back right now. In fact, he was pretty sure he never wanted to lay eyes on her again, even if he'd have to for the divorce – but he sure wished he had someone.

The concern he had heard in Zack over the phone was only amplified face-to-face. Maybe he hadn't hidden the dismay on his face well enough. "Hey, what's wrong with you?"

Dan hesitates. "Nothing man, just a lot of nothing. Let's go. I need something stronger than coffee to drink."

"Alright, hop in." He fell quiet then, working himself up to speak. They were a fair bit into the journey before he could finally finish his thought, albeit awkwardly. "Hey Dan, you know... if you need to talk, I'm listening."

Dan looked at him for a moment, considering it. People did say that a problem shared was a problem halved – but right now, he barely even wanted to think about Sarah. Having to explain what had happened all over again was not in the least bit appealing, not even if it guaranteed relief at the end. With Zack, who was clearly uncomfortable having an emotional conversation, and was just offering out of a sense of duty? Well, he didn't even have that guarantee. "Nah, I'm good. Thanks, though."

"If you're sure."

"Thanks. Hey – listen. Can I wind down a window?"

"Whatever you want, dude."

The air felt stuffy in the car now, too. It was as though Sarah was poisoning the air around him, and whenever he spent too long in the same place, it started to take on the same unpleasant quality. If that was the case, he wasn't sure what to do. He wasn't just dreading the party, now. He was dreading having to go home afterward too.

Chapter 3

When Dan arrived at the party, he had already determined that being sober was not helping him in the least. Alcohol couldn't solve every problem, and it certainly shouldn't be relied on in the long-term, but it seemed that it would help him right now. Giving weak greetings to everyone he recognized, he headed straight to the kitchen to get something to drink, hoping that it would be better than the crappy craft beer he had been expecting. When he gets to the kitchen, he sees some of his teammates standing in a loose circle, talking with someone else that he can't quite see.

Walking towards them, he hears a voice he recognizes, but can't place. When he gets to the group, he stops. Standing almost in the middle of the group talking up a storm, was Jeremy, his old captain from college. Dan just stared for a moment, looking at him. He didn't look much different from back then. Of course, he was a little older, and looked it; there was a streak of lightning to his light brown hair now, but it suited him. He obviously still worked out regularly, as his arms were well-toned, even more so than they had been back in college. The glasses he wore still gave him a slightly geeky look, but it certainly wasn't a bad effect. Dan had always liked that look.

It was best for everybody involved here if he didn't think about that. After all, Jeremy had not just been his captain.

Thankfully, there was an easy fix for this particular breed of temporary madness. He pictured his father in his head, and that was all the motivation he needed.

Beer in hand, Dan slowly backed away from the group. He was in no mood to deal with this right now. Looking back once more before leaving the room completely, he notices that Jeremy is looking right at him. He smiles at Dan but continues talking as if he had not noticed his old flame sneaking out of the room. It was frustratingly charming. Of course, Jeremy wouldn't make a fuss if he thought somebody needed to get some air. Of course, he would just let him go.

Dan headed outside to get some fresh air. May as well live in the fresh air these days, he thought, with the amount of time he spends needing it. He didn't understand why he had fled like that. Well – of course, he did, but he didn't understand why he should still have this reaction, after so many years. It was a past relationship, back when he was experimenting with the opposite sex, and that was a very long time ago now. He wasn't gay anymore, so why did he want to run out when he saw Jeremy? Why was his heart beating so fast right now?

At the end of the yard was a metal railing that looked like it was part of an unfinished fence. Dan stopped walking there and leaned against it, trying to comprehend his own actions. Almost against his will, he started thinking back to his college days and his relationship with Jeremy. It had been a great couple of years. Certainly, thinking back to those memories was better than reflecting on his marriage to Sarah; it was better than ruminating on the way she had left.

More than anything, though, he remembered the ending, and exactly how he had been forced to break Jeremy's heart.

His father was a hard-core Christian and believed that gays were all going to hell. He had been throughout Dan's whole childhood, and it was really only thanks to luck that Dan had not inherited those same views. He credited some gay friends at high school for that, as they had expanded his mind and taught him that nobody's sexuality defined them. Because of his views, however, Dan had always been forced to be very careful about what he said at home, and who he supported.

When Dan had fallen for Jeremy, that carefulness evolved fast into hiding whole parts of himself. He could barely have a conversation with his parents without feeling he was going to give himself away. It made calling home difficult and visiting home even worse. After all, when he visited, he couldn't even talk to Jeremy for support.

His father had found out entirely by mistake. Dan's parents had come to visit his college in the run-up to a big hockey game, with a view to finally taking up his offer of watching him play. He knew he'd have to be on his best behavior in order to keep his secret, and he was – but unfortunately, not all his college friends knew about his father's views. When she'd gone to introduce herself at half-time, she had unwittingly outed Dan by assuring his parents that Dan and Jeremy were a very sweet couple and totally made for each other.

Predictably, Dan's father had flipped out. There was no way he was going to let his son do that. In fact, there was no question about it; this wasn't even his son's true self. This was some kind of crazy college decision he had made without his parents' rightful influence over him like a constant shadow. In any case, he had started berating Dan with horror stories of the gay men who had attempted to play professional sports before him.

The worst part was that everything Dan's father had told him was at least partly true.

He pointed out the dichotomy between sports and mainstream society. Even though being gay was now not as big of a deal as it had been in the 60s, 70s, and 80s, this was due – according to Dan's father – to ethical degeneration. When it came to sports, the military and other tight-knit groups, where men were still men and women were still women, gays were still shunned – even beaten to death, or goaded into suicide. His father told him countless stories about such men. Some of them sounded true, and some of them less so; sometimes, however, they came backed up with newspaper clippings, and eventually Dan could no longer tell which of his father's stories was homophobic hearsay, and which were sad truths.

Even so, Dan had initially resisted walking away from the identity he had grown so comfortable with. It was then that his father had threatened to cut off paying Dan's tuition. His scholarship only covered so much of it, after all, and his parents' failure to support him would mean that he would have had to drop out of school. Even though Dan was legally old enough to make his own decisions, he soon realized he had come face to face with the horrible truth of adulthood.

Just because you were free to make your own decisions did not mean that your choices would not have consequences. Sometimes, in real life, there were no easy options; there were no nice choices.

For Dan, the thought of being unable to finish the college degree he had worked so hard for was more than he could take. It scared him to a degree he couldn't come back from, haunted by thoughts of being stuck in a dead-end office job or mired in poverty. So he had broken it off with Jeremy.

Ironic, really, that he had walked straight into professional hockey, he hadn't even needed his degree to live a successful life – but he couldn't beat himself up for that, he figured. He had made the best choice he could at the time, with the options he had. He couldn't take the risk. And who knew? Maybe his father really was right. Maybe he never would have been able to make it in professional hockey with a handsome boyfriend by his side, instead of a beautiful wife.

Even so, he knew the time after he made his choice had not been easy. He had spent numerous weeks afterward feeling low, sad… just out of it. Thinking back on it now, he kept telling himself it was just a phase that he got over it and moved on. If it had not been a phase, his life would have already come crashing down around him in spades. Hell, he was legally married to a woman. Even if the two had separated now, he had made that choice and stuck to it. He'd even been happy about it, at the time. What gay man did that?

Then he remembered; one in denial. That's what gay man did that. One who couldn't admit to himself he liked men, not women.

Chapter 4

When he saw Dan, Jeremy's heart had skipped a beat. He had known he would be at the party, considering it was his team's victory they were celebrating, but he had been so positive he was over him. They hadn't spoken since Dan had broken up with him. He didn't hold a grudge, of course. He had understood, even if it had hurt like hell. He didn't agree, not at all, but he had understood. He had just been forced to take hold of his feelings like a man and get over them – and that was exactly what he had done, so why the pulse in his chest as he saw Dan again now?

After some time, he was finally able to sneak away from the party. He had no idea where Dan had gone, so he decided to go outside for some fresh air. Walking through the front yard, Jeremy was almost knocked over by some large guy running. The guy tripped over his own feet trying to avoid the collision and landed on his rear. There was a burst of laughter from several other people who were standing close by.

The drunken guy did not look impressed. "Hey, watch where you're going next time, huh? I almost crashed into you."

Jeremy looked at him, confused but capable of standing his own ground. Despite what some bigots might have thought, Jeremy was still a hockey player despite his sexuality; there was no shortage of confidence, assertiveness, and competition in his personality. "Um, I do believe you should watch where you are going. You're the one who almost ran into me, your own words."

"Dude, what, you want a piece of me? Seriously, do you know who I am? Better think twice before running that mouth anymore."

Jeremy cocked his head to the side. "Do I know who you are? Yes, I do. You are the pompous ass that almost just ran me over. Other than that, I don't give a shit dude." He shook his head, thinking what an idiot this guy was.

The guy started towards Jeremy, obviously pissed and looking for a fight. Before he got too far, somebody was there to stop him.

Somebody Jeremy could have recognized anywhere – and who set off another pulse of electricity on Jeremy's chest.

Dan walked up from behind, grabbed his arm, wrenching it behind his back and pushing up.

"I think you might have had one too many beers, James. Why don't you go sober up somewhere before you end up sleeping face first in the grass?" Dan looked at James. This wasn't one of his teammates. Jeremy knew this from following the team – but you could tell regardless. Teammates had a certain way of dealing with each other that started with friendship and only bled into aggression if it was absolutely necessary. This guy, however, had skipped the niceties. Dan was straight onto intimidation off the bat. Maybe it was one of his teammates' friends? "Now, if I let go, you going to head on out or start more trouble?"

James glared at Dan, then Jeremy. "Nah, I'm good bro."

Dan lets go of James' arm and steps back. He's well aware of James' temper, especially when he's drinking and not taking any chances.

Sure enough, James; turns around swinging an arm towards Dan, not realizing Dan had stepped back. Because he was so drunk, he swirled around so far he was almost facing the same way when he started. There was a burst of laughter from several other people who were watching.

Dan shook his head. "James, go home. You're drunk. I'm sober. You are only going to get embarrassed. Just go home while you're ahead."

James hesitated a moment, looking around him. He realized that not only was he drunk and attempting to fight someone sober, but he was seriously outnumbered – and by big, muscular hockey players, no less.

He glared at Jeremy. "This isn't over. Watch your back asshole." Without a doubt, however, it was all hot air. The guy was wasted beyond measure, and Dan would be surprised if he remembered that any of this had happened in the morning – at least not with any great clarity.

As James stumbled off, Jeremy shook his head. "Wow, what a night."

Dan walked over to Jeremy, putting his hand on Jeremy's shoulder to steady him. He looked a little wobbly – a little vulnerable. Did he feel uncomfortable at the party now? Dan guessed he would be too if he'd just been threatened. How was Jeremy supposed to know that the other guys weren't violent? "Are you good?"

Jeremy looked Dan in the eyes. There was a strange expression there he couldn't interpret. "Yeah, I'm good. Are you?"

Dan smiled. He could only hope that their years apart had worn away at Jeremy's ability to read him because he was sure that smile wasn't very convincing. Not after Sarah – not after seeing him again after all these years. "Life goes on, I guess. You still playing hockey?"

"Oh, sure," Jeremy said, smiling faintly. "Not like you, though. I just coach at a high school not far from here."

"You didn't want to go professional?"

Jeremy wrinkled his nose. "Nah. Too much spotlight. Too much pressure. I don't think I'm cut out for that kind of life. Honestly, I don't know how you do it."

"To be honest with you, I kind of forget that anybody knows who I am," Dan admitted. "I don't even watch the games back with professional commentary if I can help it. If I thought about it all the time, I guess I'd go nuts."

"Sure would," said Jeremy. His eyes trailed over Dan, curious in a pleasant sort of way. It wasn't uncomfortable for Dan to stand there with Jeremy's gaze on him. "You know, I'm glad you're here tonight. It's been way too long since we caught up."

"It is," Dan admitted – and he wasn't sure what happened next. The words more or less jumped out of his mouth before he could stop them. "You want to go somewhere and get some drinks or maybe dinner?"

Jeremy's smile was broad and bright. Evidently, some things never changed. "I would like that, yes. That'd be nice."

"Great! I know a great little place not too far from here, although I didn't drive here, caught a ride with a friend. You?"

Jeremy laughed. "You never really did like driving anywhere. Yeah, I drove. My car's up the block a bit. Wait here and I'll go get it." He left Dan standing near the curb while he jogged up the road.

A few minutes later, he pulled up in a dark blue Mercedes sedan. Dan was impressed. Considering that Jeremy was only a high school coach, this was quite a nice car – the standard he, as a professional hockey player, was used to. When he stopped, Dan popped open the door and climbed in.

"Nice car."

Jeremy smiled. "It's my pride and joy. Now, where to?"

Chapter 5

Sitting at the two-person table at the 'Desert Rose', it felt like no time had passed at all. Any awkwardness that Dan had felt at first sight of him dissipated in the warmth of their easy chemistry. As they chatted about some of their old games when they were in college, the conversation lively and vibrant, it was almost as though the breakup and betrayal hadn't happened at all.

"You remember that time Andrew was still drunk from the night before, and he tried to convince Coach he was fine by doing a spin on the ice?"

"He ended up right on his ass."

Dan was too self-aware not to worry about irritating everybody else at the restaurant with their loud laughter, but he couldn't make himself stop. He was so carried away with Jeremy, and so excited to see him now that the initial hurdle had been surmounted, that he couldn't contain it.

"Or the game against Washington, where Ricky's parents got more wasted than he did..."

Suddenly both of them got quiet. The Washington game had been the one that changed everything for both of them, and remembering this in the middle of their friendly conversation was pretty jarring.

Dan, hating the awkward silence, finally spoke up. "Jeremy, I hope you know I am really sorry about the way things went between us. I never wanted to cause you any pain. I just..."

Jeremy reached over and put his hand on Dan's. "Shut up. I know. I know what happened and why it happened. I know all about your father and his religious crap. You warned me in the beginning he would freak out if he found out. I just didn't realize he would have so much power over you with you being an adult. But I don't hold it against you."

Dan looked at Jeremy. Just like when he was a younger man at college, he had a maturity in his expression that Dan just didn't see in other men their age, as though he'd learned and absorbed things that the rest of them missed. His heart was racing as he looked at Jeremy, and he didn't understand. He couldn't have feelings for this man. It didn't make sense after all this time – but yet, he did. He could feel that same lump in his throat he would feel in college when Jeremy was about to kiss him, even when they'd been dating for weeks. The anxiety he couldn't explain. That want that consumed him. The need, somewhere primal and deep.

Dan shook his head to clear his mind, grabbing at a painful subject just to prove his sexuality to himself – and to Jeremy, actually. It was better that there was no confusion about this, especially now they were having dinner together. "You know that I got married?"

Jeremy didn't seem surprised. "Yeah, I heard. Your name still carries weight with the old team. You can't do much more than take a piss without someone discussing it."

Dan raised his eyebrows. "Do you talk to the old players? How is everyone? Do they not have anything better to do than discuss my life?"

Jeremy laughed. "Sure they do, but you're a pro, you know? People love to shoot the shit about celebrities they used to know. Besides, they seem to think I want to hear all about you all the time. Some of them don't think I moved on, and others think you're faking your way through. I don't know. They were a crazy bunch. I am still shocked they were okay with us. Hell, Damon threw us a 'coming out' party from crying out loud."

Dan busted out with laughter. "Yeah I remember that. That was the weirdest party ever. There was way too much rainbow shit everywhere. What are we – unicorns? It was a blast, though."

"Absolutely, so – what's your wife like?"

"Um..."

Okay. This was the reason he shouldn't have brought her up. She was shorthand for saying 'I'm straight now', sure – but now he was going to have to walk through a conversational minefield to make sure he wouldn't have to tell the truth about their relationship. This was a pleasant evening; he didn't want to talk about his separation, or how she'd cleared out the apartment.

"Usually, you'd tell me she's great here, Dan."

Jeremy's smile was teasing. Clearly, he didn't realize there was anything wrong – so that, at least, was good. Dan grinned back, weakly.

"She's headstrong, definitely. Not my usual type."

When Dan stopped talking, he realized Jeremy was staring at him with that smile, the smile that said how much he still wanted Dan. Heart thumping, he realized he was wrong. He had always been wrong. He never went straight, as much as he wanted to believe it, wanted everyone else to believe it. There was no way he was even close to being straight if he still so badly needed this man sitting in front of him. He wouldn't call it love; love was too strong a word for something that had died a long time ago and had laid dormant ever since. But the potential for love was obvious. He felt things for this man even now that he had never once felt for Sarah.

Dan cleared his throat, trying to bring himself back to the present and slipping back to the subject of college hockey. "Um, yeah, good times, with the team." He looked away from Jeremy.

Jeremy couldn't believe that after what Dan had put him through, the old feelings were still there. He was still in love with him and wanted so badly to kiss him right now. But, no, he couldn't and he wouldn't. Dan had broken his heart. He wouldn't allow himself to be put through that again.

"Good times. Well, I think it's about time to call it a night, getting pretty late, after all. We're not all famous hockey players; some of us have to get up on a normal person schedule in the morning."

Dan looked back at Jeremy. "Jerk, but yeah, it is getting late, I guess." He paused, having to force himself through the next words, and not even entirely sure he wanted to say them. "So, um... I guess I will see you around? Are you staying in town or..."?

Jeremy hesitated before deciding to tell the truth. "Actually, I just moved into an apartment back in the city. I moved to coach at a new high school recently and that's where it is, so... got to stay close, you know?"

Dan smiled faintly. "Well, that's great. Boy, those kids don't know how lucky they are."

Jeremy didn't even think about it before it came out of his mouth. "Would you like to watch tryouts? They're next week."

Dan grinned. "I would love to. Here – I'll write down my cell number for you. Let me know the time and place and I will be there. I love watching the next generation learn to love hockey." He wrote his number on a napkin and handed it to Jeremy, feeling kind of like a teenager. Couldn't he just put it directly into Jeremy's phone? But Jeremy hadn't offered.

Jeremy took it and looked at it. There was an expression in his eyes that Dan couldn't read – couldn't even decide whether it was happy or sad, or somewhere in-between. It had been a long time since he'd spoken the language of Jeremy's body language, after all. He was no longer fluent.

"Okay," he said eventually. "I will talk to you soon."

He was kind enough to drop Dan back at his house, waving warmly from the window. Dan waved back, head spinning from the emotional revelations of the evening, and as though he wasn't about to walk into a bare apartment with barely any furniture in it.

He was a good guy, and it was nice to catch up with him – but that was a fact of Dan's existence that Jeremy definitely didn't need to know.

Chapter 6

For the next week, Dan went about his usual schedule. He went shopping and bought some items for the house to replace what Sarah had taken. A few dishes, a better TV and DVR setup, some furniture. He also went grocery shopping to fill the fridge and cupboards back up.

Even though he had been so pissed about her taking everything, he was actually in a really good mood. He wasn't sure why, but he thought it might have something to do with the other night and Jeremy. Maybe just knowing Jeremy didn't hate him made him feel better. If he was honest with himself, the thought of that had plagued him on many a late night, especially after he'd been drinking. He wasn't a hugely sensitive guy in the grand scheme of things, but the thought of having really torn that guy apart for no fault of his own was – well. Not a pleasant one. It was good to know that this hadn't been the case all this time.

He was walking through the boxed foods aisle at the grocery store, still somehow thinking about Jeremy when someone bumped into him. Looking up, he saw Sarah. She had some guy wrapped around her arm. It took him a second to recognize Devon, the guy she left him for. When he looked back at Sarah, she appeared to be gloating. Dan wasn't sure why this might be. Devon looked like a sewer rat's head on the body of a man taking veterinary-strength steroids – and unkind as that description was, it probably wasn't far from the truth.

"So, what are you doing here?" She said with a sneer.

Was she stupid? They were in a grocery store. What else would he be doing but buying groceries? If it was supposed to be a barb about the fact he rarely did the grocery shopping when they were together, then frankly he didn't like it. They had agreed on the division of the chores when they'd first moved in together, thinking this was the maturest way to do things. Grocery shopping had been one of hers, as his training schedule didn't leave much time to get to the store. But of course, she wouldn't be thinking about that right now.

"Well," he said, making sure to keep his voice even, "since you took it upon yourself to empty my cupboards, I thought I would fill them back up."

"Oh. I'm surprised you got off the couch long enough to go anywhere."

"What's the matter, Sarah? Are you upset because I'm not home moping about the fact that you left me for the man you cheated on me with? There, I cried for you. Happy? I have better thing to do than worry about you."

"Hey, man. That is no way to talk to a lady." Devon leaned in front of Sarah as if to protect her.

"Damn man, you're right. I will keep that in mind if I see one."

Devon balled his fists and started towards Dan. Sarah grabbed his arm. "Not here. We are in public. Besides, he's not worth it."

Dan sneered. "Yeah, neither are you. So, see ya."

He had already turned around to walk away when Devon threw a punch at his head. Dan had been hit in the head enough times playing hockey that it barely budged it, even without his helmet on. He turned around and looked Devon squarely in the face, a cool anger settling across his expression. Another thing hockey had taught him was extraordinary self-control. It would be a PR nightmare if he hit this guy back, and he had no intention of making things any worse for himself right now.

"Better think twice before doing that again. Is she really worth it? You do know that a cheater will always be a cheater, right?"

Devon hesitated long enough for Sarah to get a better grip on him. "C'mon. Let's go, baby."

Devon let Sarah drag him away, but glared at Dan the whole time that he could see him. Dan stood there for a moment, trying to calm back down. Neither one of them was worth a night in jail, or the media outrage. He had to just keep repeating that to himself until he believed it – until the anger died down, and he could see again until the red mist lifted.

He finally got himself under control and finished his shopping. While he was loading up his car, someone tapped him on the shoulder. It caught him off guard enough he turned around with his fists ready, too worked up with the violence he'd already experienced today.

Luckily, Jeremy stepped back before Dan could swing. "Hey man, whoa. I come in peace."

Dan caught himself and stopped, embarrassed to have overreacted so badly. It was Jeremy – not an enemy. Work it out, brain. He took a deep breath and let it out, exhaling in one big, heavy stream. "Sorry, man. It's been a hell of a day."

Jeremy nodded, turning back to the store. He looked concerned. "Did I just see your wife with another guy in there?"

Well. He couldn't get away from it now. He had to explain to Jeremy.

"Yes," he said eventually. "You did. She walked out on me a few days ago. Apparently, I'm disconnected, and, uh... I guess I don't look like the deflated animal-shaped balloon she's walking around with instead? I don't know. It's still news to me."

Jeremy stayed quiet for a while; turning back towards Dan and helping him lift his groceries into the car. "I'm sorry about that, Dan."

He shook his head. He really didn't want anybody to feel sorry for him. Even if it sucked right now, he knew it would be a good thing in the long-term, and that was what they should all be focusing on, he figured. "It's fine, really. I think maybe it's been a long time coming."

"You should have said the other night," Jeremy insisted, lifting the last bag of groceries in for him. "There I was, asking all about her..."

"I brought her up," he assured him, closing the trunk of the car. "And thanks."

"No problem," said Jeremy, rubbing his hands together now that they were empty. "So... I take it that was the 'hell' part of your day?"

"Close enough. We crossed paths in the store and her junked-up weasel thought he'd take a swing at me."

"Seriously?" said Jeremy, eyes wide. "Jesus Christ. You should have called security."

"Probably," Dan reasoned, "but I really don't need the story breaking in the national media right now. You know they love a sports star with marital problems. I just told him to back down, and he did."

"Sure, but people like that need to know they can't just hit people in public. I mean – what was he thinking? He should at least be banned from the store."

Dan nodded. "Oh yeah, definitely, but I'm good now. What are you doing here?"

"Well, from the looks of it, the same thing you were attempting to do. I needed a few things from the store. Since this one is walking distance from my apartment, I figured I would come see whether it was worth a damn."

"Well, before today, I would have said yeah, it was a pretty good place. I know the manager and he is good with ordering specialty items for customers. But, that was before today. At the moment, I can't say – unless you like the idea of being assaulted in the aisles."

Jeremy just looked at Dan. He could tell that last part was a joke, but he was a bit concerned about him. He seemed really agitated about his wife. He wondered if he still had feelings for her or if he was just pissed at the situation. Trying to think of something to take Dan's mind off it, he shrugged. No time like the present to get his feelings hurt.

"Dan, would you like to come over for dinner? If you're busy, it's fine, but I thought, well, maybe you could use a friend tonight."

Dan looked at Jeremy hard. Was he really just concerned, or was it something else? And was this really a good idea either way? Like Jeremy said, though, he could probably use some company tonight. He really was still reeling from the breakdown of his marriage, and even though he'd tried his best to fill it, the apartment didn't exactly feel homey right now. In the end, it felt like the choice was already made for him. "Um, no, I'm not busy. Dinner sounds good, actually. Where?"

"Here's my address. Say around 6ish?" He pulled out a small notepad from his pocket and wrote on it, then handed it to Dan. Dan could see the edge of the napkin he'd scribbled his number on sticking out of the edge of Jeremy's pocket, not yet removed. "Are you going to be able to find it, or do you need directions?"

Dan looked at the slip of paper now, noting the address. "Actually, I know exactly where this is. An old friend of mine lives a couple doors down. So, I will see you around 6. Do I need to bring anything? Dessert, drinks?"

"Um, you can if you want, sure. I'll see you then." Jeremy smile. He still didn't know what the hell he was doing. He should probably be staying as far away from Dan as possible, at least when it came to more intimate settings like this. But he couldn't seem to do it. Well, he would just see how the night went. It was just as friends, right? They were grown men. They could keep it that way.

Chapter 7

Dan showed up a few minutes early, having spent the entire afternoon too jumped-up to wait any longer. He was so tightly wound that he didn't pay attention to the address, and almost knocked on the wrong house – but thankfully he realized his mistake at the last second, and veered over to Jeremy's instead. When he finally arrived at the right place and confirmed from the note that it was Jeremy's, he was so nervous he almost dropped the bottle of champagne and store-bought pie he had brought. Holding on to it with a renewed strength in his grip, he knocked on the door somewhat louder than he intended. What the hell was wrong with him? This was just dinner between two old friends, nothing more. But, then why did he feel like a teenager picking up his prom date?

He hadn't even felt this chewed up at his actual prom.

Jeremy opened the door and looked at Dan. His heart melted. Dan was wearing dark slacks that fit him perfectly and a light blue dress shirt that showed off his muscular arms. His hair was combed forward and slightly up into a quiff as he'd always worn at college – at least after he'd learned how to do it – and it made Jeremy want to grab him and drag him to bed on some primal level, even if his conscious mind knew that this would be a totally terrible idea. Nor would Dan go for it if he even asked. Instead, he smiled at Dan and asked him to come in.

"I will say that you do look nice. Are you going somewhere after dinner?"

Dan laughed. "Um, no, I really didn't know what to wear and I wasn't spending half the night in the closet like a girl trying to pick something. So I just grabbed some nice clothes and, voila."

Jeremy felt a bit under-dressed compared to Dan. He was wearing a pair of loose blue jeans and a t-shirt that said 'I'm not anti-social, I'm anti-stupid'. He had just grabbed it and threw it on. He was too busy cooking to think about wardrobe. Oh well, too late now. He just hoped that Dan didn't feel self-conscious or over-dressed. Clearly, he looked good enough to excuse any misjudgment about the tone of the evening.

Dan was trying to not watch Jeremy. He looked pretty hot in those jeans. Dan shook his head. No. He knew now that he wasn't straight, but he still had to act as though he was. He was a professional sports player, and he had to be very clear on his stance, both internally and with everybody else – guys were not attractive. Jeremy was the only person that threatened this status quo anyway, so exactly how gay could he realistically be?

Damn, tonight was a bad idea.

He looked at Jeremy in the eyes. For a few long seconds, he was about to tell him that he had to go when Jeremy smiled. It was too bright and sincere to handle, so he had to change his mind. Yeah, he was staying. There was no way he could skip out on him again, not even just for an evening. The damage had already been done once, and he didn't want to reopen the wound – especially seeing as Jeremy had been so kind to invite him over in the first place.

"So, what's for dinner?"

Jeremy cocked his head to the side. "Um, food."

Dan just looked at him. He always was a smart ass. "Really? That sense of humor's still sticking around, huh? You haven't learned any real jokes yet?"

Jeremy laughed, leading him through to the dining room. "You're getting chili lime steak with honeyed carrots and roasted bell peppers."

Dan couldn't help but be impressed. Of course, he hadn't tasted it yet, but purely on the description, it sounded like restaurant food. He himself had never been able to cook anything fancy. All previous attempts, for anniversaries and the like, had ended in consummate disaster. "Oh, well, that sounds different. It's delicious but different."

"You'll love it, I'm sure. It's my specialty. Do I see dessert in that bag you're carrying there like you said? What did you bring?"

"I brought a bottle of champagne and a peach pie."

"You brought champagne, huh? Fame really changed you." Jeremy grinned. "I love peach. It's my favorite fruit. Here, set it down right here in the middle."

"Yeah, I figured," Dan admitted. "I remembered how much you loved peach, uh... well. Peach everything. So I figured I couldn't go wrong with it."

"You're damn right," Jeremy assured him, eyes fixed on the pie as it was brought out of the bag. "Oh, it's going to be so hard to finish dinner now. All I'm going to think about is that dessert."

"See – you can't say I didn't contribute."

Jeremy looked at Dan. There was a twinkle in his eyes. "Thanks. So, um, well the food is ready. You want to go ahead and eat or would you like to have drinks first?"

"Actually, I'm starved. Let's eat."

Jeremy laughed. "Sounds great, dinner's on."

If there had been any tension when Dan was considering turning on his heel and walking away, it had completely disappeared now. Just like it had in the restaurant, their chemistry had won out, papering over any awkwardness that remained between them, that, at least, Dan could be grateful for.

Chapter 8

"My god," said Jeremy, a few minutes in. "I know I said you were going to enjoy it, but you've almost finished."

"You're a good cook," Dan said, sheepish at the amount he'd already cleared off his plate. "This is really good. You're going to have to make it for me again."

For all Dan's anxiety about it, the meal was going exceptionally well. They chatted a lot about what had happened in their lives during the last few years. Dan learned that Jeremy had gone to Costa Rica for a year, and came back fluent in Spanish; he described his own solid commitment to his team, and how it had more or less eaten up the past few years of his life. He mostly tried to avoid talking about his marriage as much as possible, but eventually, he could avoid the subject no longer.

"My father brought her and her mother to the house one day during a party he was throwing. He loved to throw those damn parties. Showing off his wealth, you know? Use to drive me crazy as a kid, but I grew used to them by the time I was an adult. Anyway, the father had brought them to this party, unknown to me, to meet me. She sees me, walks right up to me and says, 'You're mine tonight,' grabs my hand and drags me to the center of the room. I was fairly lit by then and just went with it."

Jeremy grinned at him, eyes slightly narrowed in judgment as he pressed for more details. "So... what, you married her because she had balls?"

It was shamefully close to the truth, now that he thought about it.

"No. Yes. I don't know. She proposed to me, not the other way around. I had been bouncing around relationships, never staying more than a couple days in it, and she was, well, I couldn't shake her. No matter how hard I tried. So, I said, why not?"

Jeremy wasn't normally a sarcastic guy, but it was heavy in his voice now as he sipped his champagne. "Wow, Dan. That's a great reason to get married."

"No, I know it wasn't. I was stupid, but... I thought I really loved her, obviously. I thought that was what adults did, you know? I thought we all settled down with the women that could tolerate us, and... well. Clearly, she was happy to have me. I just never stopped to think about whether I actually liked her; I doubt she stopped to think about whether she actually liked me. Hell, I barely tolerated her when I was sober. But, it made a father happy, so..."

"I see. And to keep getting money, you got to keep daddy happy."

Dan's smile faltered. He wasn't sure what to say. That comment hurt, but it was the truth. Maybe it hurt because it was the truth. When he was younger, that was what he cared about, the money. It was why he had left Jeremy to begin with – but he desperately wanted to clarify that this wasn't a light decision. He hadn't just chosen money over Jeremy as a vague concept. He had needed the money to finish college. It wasn't to support a champagne lifestyle, or for the status – nothing like that. Was that genuine reason not enough? Jeremy had always maintained that he understood why Dan had been backed into a corner, and understood that he didn't really have a choice.

Dan looked at him now, the man that he had cared about all of those years ago. How could he ever make up for it? How does one mend a broken heart?

"I am sorry, Dan. I didn't mean to say it like that."

Dan forced a smile. "No, don't worry about it. Sometimes the truth hurts." He hesitated before going on. "Jeremy, I am the one who should be sorry. What happened back then was wrong. I shouldn't have let my father's money control me. I mean maybe I could have found another way to pay my tuition costs. You must think I was spoiled, a spoiled brat."

Jeremy smiled at him. "Dan, it's okay. I know why you did it, I understand. Yes, it hurt. Yes, you broke my heart. But, you didn't really have a lot of other options. I don't know if you remember, but I do. We looked into aid, which you weren't eligible for. We worked everything out. Keeping up with your college tuition would have meant you had to get a job, and you wouldn't have had time to study, work and play hockey – and how could I have asked you to give up on your hockey?"

He paused, and they looked at each other. Dan felt the ghost of the forced decision settle on the back of his neck, still heavy and unpleasant after all these years.

"It's okay," said Jeremy, and he certainly sounded sincere. "It's done and over with, in the past. Let's move on and talk about something else. I'm sorry my sentence came out like that."

Dan looked at Jeremy. "Okay, moving on."

"Good."

"So," he said, searching quickly for a topic of conversation. One stuck out to him – one that wouldn't go away, no matter how hard he tried to find something else. Eventually, he realized that he couldn't escape it. Some part of him really badly wanted to know, and it wouldn't give up until he asked. "Have you had any meaningful relationships? Hopefully, you had something better than me and Sarah."

Jeremy shook his head. "No. I just haven't met anyone I thought was worth the time. Well, I mean, I have met a couple of guys that I really liked, but, I don't know, just wasn't interested in something long term. But I did meet this one girl. We became really good friends. We hang out; go see a movie once in a while, mostly when she's between boyfriends, which is often."

Dan was shocked. "A girl? Really?"

"It's not like that. She really is just a friend, but a good friend, like a sister, maybe. She knows I'm gay, even if I am quiet about it. I like hanging out with her. She likes hanging out with me. There's nothing else, so get that look off your face."

Dan tried to look innocent. "What look? I didn't give a look. But I think it is awfully funny."

Jeremy laughed at Dan. He thought he was so cute when he made weird faces.

When dinner was over, both of them grabbed dishes to take to the kitchen. Jeremy told Dan that he was a guest and, therefore, did not have to help clean up. Dan just smiled at Jeremy and did it anyway. He knew Jeremy wasn't passive-aggressive like Sarah, but it had been worn into him for years now – whether or not somebody refused help with the dishes, they still wanted help with the dishes, and you were best off offering a hand. In any case, it got the job done faster. Afterward, they took drinks to the living room. Dan sat on one side of the large couch and Jeremy on the other.

Dan finally broke the companionable silence that had settled in as they finished their champagne. He'd probably had too much of it this evening – evidenced by the fact that he actually up and said what he was thinking right now, with no pause for thought. "Jere, I have to say that... even though I know this was just supposed to be two old friends catching up, it feels more like a date. Maybe it's because of our history as a couple, but, well. I don't know where exactly I was going with that. Just felt like I should probably say it out loud."

Jeremy hesitated a few moments before speaking his mind. "Dan, I don't know what to say. I... well I still have feelings for you. I don't want to. I keep hoping that they will go away with time, that we can be just friends. But... well, it's going to be a lot harder than I anticipated."

Dan looked down at his lap, head fuzzy with the champagne. It was stronger than he remembered. "Yeah, I know. I, um, well. I don't know what to say. I honestly don't deserve your friendship, but I will settle for it. I couldn't ask you for more than that."

Jeremy looked at Dan hard. Trying to study his face, he was confused. Was Dan saying he still had feelings for him as well? And if so, then what? Jeremy wasn't sure he could ever trust Dan again, but he wanted to. He wanted to grab his face and kiss him, a deep passionate kiss. But he held back.

Dan looked up at Jeremy. Jeremy could see the hurt in his eyes, and noticing it, he couldn't resist anymore. He slid over to Dan and put his hands on each side of Dan's face. Dan looked at Jeremy for only a moment more before leaning in closer and putting his lips on Jeremy's.

With that, the spell was broken. There was no pretense left – no barrier between them. Their chemistry was spilling over, and intense enough to overcome any obstacles that Dan had left. If his father was still a voice in the back of his head, then that voice was remarkably quiet as they kissed now. Besides, the night was still young – and judging by the strength of that chemistry, kissing wouldn't be the last thing they did.

Chapter 9

The next morning, Dan woke first. He looked around for a moment before remembering where he was – but surprisingly enough, when he worked it out, the shock didn't throw him off at all. He smiled. Looking beside him, he noticed Jeremy was still asleep. He thought about getting up but decided against it. It wouldn't help gain Jeremy's trust again if he seemed to be sneaking out of the bed. Instead, he rolled over and got closer to Jeremy, throwing an arm over his bare shoulders. Bending up his arm, he gently ran his fingers through Jeremy's salt-and-pepper hair. A feeling of happiness surged through him and he wanted this moment to last forever. But he knew all good things must end eventually.

Jeremy finally opened his eyes and looked into Dan's. He smiled. "Good morning gorgeous. How did you sleep?"

"Well, your bed is very lumpy and you snore awful loud."

Jeremy faked a look of shock, sleepy enough to be childish and playful. "Oh, yeah. Well, you kick like a mule and fart like a buffalo. So there."

Dan busted out laughing. "Whatever. You're full of shit."

Jeremy laughed with him, snuggling up closer towards him. "No, I am not. You're a damn bully. But I bet you're still a ticklish bully."

Dan started scooting out of the bed quick. "Don't you dare. I will start kicking like a mule." He was laughing so hard that he wasn't paying attention to how close to the edge he was until it was too late. He fell to the floor with a hard thump and laughed even harder.

Jeremy jumped to the edge near Dan to help him up. Between laughs, he offered to help. Once he was up, they both agreed on a shower. Unable to decide who would go first, they decided to take one together. Needless to say, this was a decision they did not regret.

After they were done and washed, then dried and dressed again, Dan went into the kitchen to find something to make them for breakfast. Jeremy came in not long after and just sat down at the table. He watched Dan mess around in the kitchen, making omelets.

While he watched, he thought about their previous relationship. It had been so great. Jeremy had been staying in a dorm room, but Dan had an actual apartment, which is where they had stayed most of the time. Though they'd only been college students, weeks into puppy love and with no real-world experience, they had felt so domestic there together, sharing chores and spending their evenings piled up on the couch, so comfortable and fond of one another that it felt like home.

Then he remembered the day that Dan had broken up with him. They had been seeing each other for almost a year by that point, but after Dan's father found out, all that they'd worked for over those twelve great months had faded away in the space of a few hours. He had come over to Dan's and found his stuff in boxes.

Jeremy shook his head to clear the bad memories. He didn't want to think about them. Clearly, however, Dan saw this gesture and looked at him searchingly.

"Are you okay? You look upset."

Jeremy forced a small smile. "Just thinking."

"Well," said Dan, taking a few steps closer, the spoon from the jelly in his mouth. "Tell me your thoughts. Don't be a stranger."

He felt a little less enthusiastic about hearing those thoughts as he spent more time examining the look on Jeremy's face. It took a long while for him to speak – and as any adult knew, that didn't bode well. "Look, I had a great time last night and this morning. But I just can't go through the past again. I can't go through that pain again. So this was a one-time thing, okay?"

Dan gave a small nod, incapable of fighting off the hurt, but at least struggling to keep the majority of it off his face. This was Jeremy's decision to make, and he should have expected it after what had happened at college. Hadn't he been surprised all this time that Jeremy seemed not to be harboring any discomfort with him at all? There had to be some effect of his betrayal still in Jeremy's life – and now, he had found it. It was here, now that they'd crossed this line.

"Yeah, Jere, I understand. If that's how you want it, then I won't argue. After breakfast, I will head out, okay?"

Jeremy looked at him. Once again, Dan couldn't read the look on his face. He wished that he could. "Yeah, you can still come to tryouts, though. Tryouts are tomorrow afternoon, at 3."

"I'll be there."

Dan turned around and finished the food. They both sat and ate in silence, kind conversation killed by the knowledge that this couldn't continue. As good as it was, it was carrying too much of the past on its shoulders. After all, no matter how great a relationship was, there were some things you just couldn't forget about or walk away from.

Chapter 10

The next day, Dan showed up on time for tryouts. He enjoyed watching kids play the game, and seeing them fall in love with the drills, and the teamwork, and the strategy. Strategy for hockey looked deceptively simple; underneath the surface, there were whole worlds of things to learn, and it was thrilling to see people begin to scratch the surface on that – to realize that they had so much more to explore in this sport than they already had. Besides, they weren't nearly as brutal as the older guys were on professional teams. In college, they started getting pretty rough, but even they didn't compare to the pros. It made him miss high school and college teams.

Jeremy was already on the ice when he arrived, walking around and checking for cracks or other damage to the ice. A small chunk of ice could be more than enough to send a team member flying or fly up and hit someone. Hockey was a dangerous game, even if it didn't involve the brutality. Dan watched him as he would bend over here or there, double checking different sections. The kids were walking around the seating, looking seriously bored. He guessed this part wasn't nearly as exciting as playing.

When Jeremy was satisfied the ice was as safe as it would get, he blew the whistle around his neck. All of the kids looked up, seen him waving at them and came running to the edge. He started talking to them about the safety rules and other stuff. Dan just sat there and watched, grinning at the bored expressions on their faces. They must have heard this a thousand times now, but they'd have to get used to it. They'd hear it at least a thousand times more if they wanted to stick with the sport – and of course, he hoped that some of them did.

Eventually, his mind started wandering, and he thought about the other night with Jeremy. He had felt so alive, happy. But he had hurt Jeremy once before. He didn't blame him for wanting to keep him at an arm's length. If the situation was reversed, he guessed that he would feel the same. He wondered if there would ever be a chance to fix it and make the relationship work. Then he wondered if Jeremy would even give it a chance.

After all, he could probably have any guy he wanted. Why would he risk everything for Dan?

Jeremy loved teaching kids. It was what he had gone to college for, to be a teacher. It just turned out that he loved the sport enough that it turned into his focus instead. He had always loved kids, teaching them, watching them learn new things. It amazed him and filled him with joy. It also gave him a chance to be a kid again too. Today, however, he was distracted. He knew Dan was in the stands, he had seen him enter. He kept thinking about the other night and the morning after. He felt that he had been so rude, especially to a guy that clearly needed support right now, but he had to be strong to defend himself against the same old heartache.

Frankly, he knew he was taking a big chance by letting himself even think about a relationship with Dan. God forbid he should get attached to the idea so that he couldn't walk away from it – but he couldn't help himself. Those feelings were so strong. Something told him that they were supposed to find each other again, with years between them as a buffer. Some small, rebellious part of him hated the idea that Dan's father should win this scenario.

Undoubtedly, he was winning right now. His son was outwardly straight and married to a woman – who he clearly didn't like, and who didn't like him. The boyfriend that had threatened the family's traditional values was out of the picture and had been for years. He probably thought the battle was over now, and that he was right about Dan's sexuality being a phase. Was it Jeremy's job to help restart that war, and let the right side win at last?

Luckily for him, he had a team captain to decide who to take on the team and who to cut because he had missed quite a bit. Aaron, the captain, walked up to him after tryouts and asked him if he was okay.

"What do mean? Yeah, I'm fine. Why?"

"Well, you were somewhere else this whole time. You weren't paying any kind of attention. I was just worried you might be getting sick or something. You never miss the chance to yell at someone during these things."

Jeremy smiled at him. "Yeah, okay Aaron. Yes, I was distracted. But I'm fine. Not sick or anything, just, distracted."

Aaron looked at him seriously. "Want to talk about it? I have known you for a couple of years now. It would take something pretty serious to keep your attention this bad."

Jeremy couldn't help but to look up at Dan sitting in the bleachers still. Dan waved when he saw Jeremy looking at him.

Aaron saw it as well. "Ah, I see. Is he new?"

Jeremy looked at Aaron. "No. Unfortunately, he is not. That is Dan, from college."

Aaron looked confused for a moment. Then his face lit up. "Wait a minute, the one that got away? Broke your heart for money? What is he doing here?"

Jeremy smiled crookedly. "I invited him, just as friends."

Aaron mashed his lips together and just nodded. He knew better than to argue.

Chapter 11

After tryouts, Dan caught up with Jeremy. "Hey, I just wanted to thank you for still letting me come. That was great. You did seem distracted, but I loved it. The kids are great. How do you decide who to keep?"

"Usually, Aaron and I agree on who stays and who goes. This is his first time deciding on his own, but I figure he did a pretty good job."

"You think he'll go on to play at college?"

"Oh, most definitely," said Jeremy, watching the kids skate off. "I think a few of them will, honestly, but Aaron really has that commitment, you know? I think he could go all the way – but I guess you'd know that better than I would."

They smiled at each other, suddenly awkward, and Dan was forced to scramble for something to say just to interrupt the silence.

"Ah. Well, I had a great time. Thanks. I will go away now, leave you be."

"Dan, wait. Let's go talk. Okay?"

Dan hesitates for a moment. He really didn't want to be reminded of how much of an ass he was in college. But after seeing the look on Jeremy's face, he couldn't resist.

"Okay, where to?"

Give me a minute and we can walk over to the café. They have decent coffee and I could use some."

Dan pitched in and helped Jeremy put up the equipment. It felt good to be on the ice away from his team duties, honestly. It felt like a hobby again. Once they finished, Jeremy put his clipboard and whistle in his office and locked the door. They headed over to the café that was next to the school. It was usually the teacher hangout, but quite a few students would come and sit to do homework before going home – and of course there were other clients, too.

When they arrived, there were only a couple of other people there, so they had their pick of seating. Choosing a booth near the back but close to a window, Jeremy slid in and waited for Dan to get situated.

"Alright, so I have been thinking."

"Oh, that's a scary thought."

Jeremy smiled at Dan. "You always have to be a smart ass, don't you?"

"Sure, why not? Maybe it will lighten the mood a bit. You look too serious."

Jeremy shook his head while laughing. "Yeah, okay. Maybe you're right. But to me, this is a bit serious. Dan, I can't be friends with you. Yes, you hurt me, but it was a long time ago and I'm over it. But, I... just can't be just friends. Those feelings never went away. And I don't want another heartbreak. So I am at a loss as to what to do."

Dan just stares at Jeremy. He had expected the 'let's not be friends' part, but not the rest. Was Jeremy saying he was still in love with him? He was unsure of what to do here.

Jeremy looks at him. "So, say something. Help me figure this out. Tell me what is going on in that brain of yours. Was the other night just a fling, for old time's sake? If so, that's fine. But I need to know now, I can't keep guessing."

Dan opened his mouth to speak, but the words were not coming out. He looked at Jeremy and let his mind run. After a moment, he finally knew what he needed and wanted to say.

"Jeremy, I really, really like you. I loved you then and I think I could love you even more now – now that we're... you know. We're older – more developed. I see things in you I like so much, and..." he trailed off, realizing he was talking too much. Move on, Dan. "I made a huge mistake back then; I should never have let someone else tell me how I felt. I knew how I felt, but I was stupid and young. But I'm not young anymore and no one tells me what I can and cannot do, period. I loved the other night and enjoyed the next morning even more. Waking up next to you, seeing you smile at me first thing in the morning was the greatest pleasure I have ever known. I would love to have that every day.

"But I would understand if you can't do that. What I did, no matter how much we talk about... no, having no options, and the fact you understood, and all that... it feels like it was unforgivable. And I could never hold it against you for hating me for it if you ever did. But, if you can see it give me a chance, I promise you, I will never leave you again. No one will ever come between us, not on my part. I will make you glad you choose to give us a second chance. But if you don't want it, I promise to leave you alone. I would never..."

Before he could keep talking, Jeremy jumped up and leaned over the table. He grabbed Dan's face and pulled it close so he could kiss him, soft and sweet for a public place. Everything Dan had said had been exactly what Jeremy wanted to hear, and then some. He had not been able to quit thinking about the other day either.

Dan finally pulled away a little, his grin dizzy and delighted. "I guess this is a yes? If so, uh... can we go somewhere a bit more private?"

Jeremy smiled. "Should we go to my place?"

Dan smiled back. "That sounds perfect."

"Sure," said Jeremy. "Just let me get a few things from my office? You can wait here. I'll be literally five minutes, I swear."

"Hey, no," said Dan, unable to wipe the smile off his face. "Take your time."

After all, there was nothing in-between them now. They had all the time in the world. He watched him leave, seeing him walk away across the street and towards the school with a noticeable spring in his step – and then he heard the sound of somebody sitting in the chair opposite.

"Oh, sorry," he started, turning around to offer them the table. "Do you need-"

He cut himself off. This was not a busy punter looking for a table. This was somebody else entirely – somebody he really, really didn't want to see right now.

"I need answers," said his wife Sarah, her voice a false, sickly-sweet chirp. "That's what I need from you right now. So exactly who was that?"

"You know we're separated, right?" he said, heart hammering in his chest as he tried to avoid the upcoming conversation. "We're not a thing anymore."

"I think I deserve to know if my husband has been gay this entire time."

"I really don't see how it's any of your business what I do or don't feel," he told her coolly, trying to project an air of confidence. He didn't want to give her a direct answer at all, but it surprised him to find that this was more because he didn't want to talk to her in the first place – not because he was ashamed. "You're with that knuckle-dragging baseball gorilla of yours now."

"And you're with... a man."

Dan shrugged, incapable of dodging the question anymore. "So what if I am?"

"I'll tell you so what," she said, leaning in closer. "I think Perez Hilton would like to hear about that. And Entertainment Weekly, and USA Today, and People magazine, and..."

"Are you threatening me?" he said, with an air of boredom about him. "Or blackmailing me, or just trying to upset me? What?"

His apathy surprised her. Clearly, she had been expecting to frighten him with what she said, for whatever purpose, and seeing that he wasn't scared at all was throwing her off. "Do you honestly think your teammates are still going to want to play with you when they find this out? Share a changing room with you? I could ruin your career."

"Go right ahead," he told her simply. "I'm sure they'll run the story. You're right; the magazines would probably want to know. By the way – did you hear Gawker's filing for bankruptcy?"

"What does that have to do with anything?"

"Gawker is filing for bankruptcy," he told her, "because they're getting their asses sued off 'cos they outed a gay man. I really hope that doesn't put a dampener on your efforts to sell your story. What do you think?"

She scowled. Not for the first time, Dan realized that there was nothing about her which he missed; there was no part of their relationship that he was mourning.

He smiled back at her, bright and easy. "Tell whoever you like, Sarah. I have CCTV footage of you taking property I paid for from our house, and I'm sure if I looked back on the camera I'd find CCTV footage of your baseball jerk coming over long before we broke up. Wouldn't I?"

"I..."

"It's your choice, Sarah," he said. "I'm not interested in starting a fight with you, but rest assured. If you start one, I will end it – and being gay isn't a bad thing, you know. Being a long-term cheater and gold-digger really is."

She pursed her lips, standing up from the table. "I do not appreciate you threatening me."

"We both know I'm not threatening you, Sarah. It's just that you failed miserably to threaten me. So why don't you go and tell whoever you like about me dating a man? You'll be signing the divorce papers soon anyway."

When Jeremy got back from his office, Dan realized he must have one hell of a grin on his face. Jeremy gave him a funny look, smile twitching onto his lips. "What? Did something happen?"

"Let's drive home," he said. "I'll tell you in the car."

Chapter 12

When they finally arrived at Jeremy's apartment, having laughed at Sarah all the way – and having impressed Jeremy with his confidence – they could wait for each other no longer. They barely got in the door without stripping each other in the hallway. They had been fondling each other almost the entire trip, even throughout Dan's story about Sarah. Dan pulled Jeremy's pants off and then almost tripped on them. Jeremy busted out laughing so Dan went down to the floor and drug Jeremy with him. Both of them were laughing so hard they had to stop kissing.

Jeremy managed to stop laughing first. "You want to go to the bedroom?"

Dan had to catch his breath. After a moment, he finally was able to. "Why? You have a perfectly good floor, couch, and counter."

Jeremy leaned in to kiss him again. Their already-hard cocks bumped up against one another as they stepped in close, as eager for one another as it was possible to be. It felt like it had been so long since they'd slept together after dinner, and in the shower; it felt like they had waited since college all over again. Thankfully, now, they didn't have to wait anymore.

Jeremy slipped to his knees as Dan took a seat on the couch, grinning up at Dan's slack-jawed excitement. His hands ran over Dan's thighs, smoothing over the skin there and enjoying the way it made his hairs stand up. Before long, he couldn't ignore the bulge in his boxers anymore, and tugged those down too, letting Dan's cock spring free from its confines.

"God, Jeremy," said Dan, voice thick with desire. "Please."

Jeremy's grip was strong around the base of his length, mouth hot and warm around the rest of him. He was too big to take all the way, but Jeremy didn't seem to mind; he was even better than he had been in college, his tongue masterful on the underside of Dan's cock, and when

Dan came it felt like falling upwards into space, with only Jeremy's hands firm against him to anchor him down to earth.

"You're unbelievable," he told him, drowsy with lust, and sat up to give him a long, heady kiss. Jeremy climbed into his lap, hands all over the toned expanse of Dan's chest, and eventually the light rub of Jeremy's ass against him had Dan hard all over again.

Jeremy moaned quietly, nuzzling up into Dan's throat. "I want you," he told him. And how could Dan ignore a blatant request like that?

He had him there on the couch after Jeremy had run to pick up a condom and some lube. Jeremy was heavy and handsome in his lap, riding up and down on Dan's cock with youthful eagerness. The other night, they had done this the other way round; Jeremy had kept him pinned and fucked him into the mattress, letting him keen and buck and whine his way to oblivion. It had been so many years since Dan had slept with a man like this, and it took his breath away to feel Jeremy's tightness around him. It didn't take long for either of them to spill over the edge moans loud enough for the neighbors to hear them, and barely even caring that it was the case.

Nothing really mattered anymore except the way Jeremy made him feel – not just in sex, but in general. There were no spaces left between them. They were back to the way things were at college, only infinitely better. Dan wasn't afraid anymore. There was absolutely nothing that could come between them and scare him back away.

Undoubtedly it would be tough if – or rather, when – Sarah spoke to the media, but they'd get through it together. Neither of them doubted that.

Later, after they had sex several times and were both out of breath and energy, they lay side by side in bed, Dan lying in the crook of Jeremy's arm. He couldn't think of anywhere he would rather be right now, or ever for that matter.

Jeremy was smiling so hard his cheeks hurt a little. "So, now what?"

"Now, nothing, just relax and enjoy the quiet. I'm starving, you?"

"After that workout, hell yeah, you want me to fix us something to eat?"

"No, Jere. I want you to lay here and relax. I got it."

"Since when did you know how to cook?"

"Hey, I have learned a lot in the last few years. So shut up and sit there."

Jeremy laughed, "Yes, massa, whatever you say, massa."

Dan threw a throw pillow at him. "Shush. I'll be back." He was laughing too. He walked into the kitchen to see what Jeremy had in the cupboards. He was surprised that there was quite a bit – but then, he supposed he shouldn't be after their dinner party. That was just another thing to get excited about, he supposed. That chili and lime steak had tasted incredible. What else did Jeremy have up his culinary sleeve? Browsing around with far less skill on his side, he decided to settle for making a simple grilled egg, bacon and cheese sandwiches. That, at least, he couldn't screw up.

As he pulled out the ingredients and set them on the counter, though, he noticed a piece of paper sticking out of a drawer. Being his nosy self, he pulled it out to see what it was – though he knew fine well that he shouldn't.

It had a Duke University logo on it. When he opened it, he knew what it was. The college was offering Jeremy a job, with a nice salary. He was confused. Why would Jeremy want to work out a relationship with him here if he was moving several states away? Then it clicked. Maybe he was getting even with Dan. And what better way to do it.

He put the letter back and finished making breakfast. He tried to keep calm but it was hard, knowing fine well that this wasn't the permanent new fixture in his life he thought it was. He'd come out to Sarah for this? When he brought the food back to Jeremy, he had a sour enough look on his face that Jeremy knew something was wrong.

"Dan, what's wrong?"

Dan hesitated, but it didn't take long for him to speak. Screw it. If Jeremy really was getting even, he wanted it to be done and over with.

"Why didn't you tell me you were moving to North Carolina?"

At first, Jeremy looked confused. Then he remembered the letter in the kitchen and busted out laughing. He knew exactly what was going on.

"Dan, baby, first off, you shouldn't be snooping. God only knows it'll get you in worse trouble than this someday. Second, I'm not moving anywhere. If you would have been paying attention instead of freaking out straight away, you would have also found my rejection letter that was with it. I already typed it up, but I just hadn't sent it in yet. I wanted to find out for sure whether we were going to work or if this was a game. If it wasn't serious, then, yeah, I was going to go. But I'm not, so... you really need to take a break and calm down."

Dan looked at Jeremy for a moment, red mist falling in seconds. It was all a misunderstanding. Had he really just risked this relationship for the sake of not reading the second letter?

"Oh. Well, I guess that's what I get for being nosy."

"You didn't honestly think I would do that to you, did you? I thought you knew I wasn't a vengeful person."

Dan smiled. "I apologize. I guess it was that guilty conscious of mine. I'm glad you're not going."

"Well, I am too – even if my boyfriend is an invasive jerk. Now climb in here with me and let's eat. It looks delicious but I bet it's getting cold."

Sheepish, Dan climbed in beside him, letting the plate settle between them. "I don't deserve you, Jeremy. I really don't."

"Well, maybe not," said Jeremy, voice playful enough that Dan knew he didn't mean it. "But I figure you spent enough years married to that bitch Sarah that you've kind of evened out."

Dan laughed, picking up one of the sandwiches to take a bite. "Well, thanks, how generous." The sandwich was just the same as he'd always made it at home, but for some reason, it tasted so much better right now. Everything was right in his life. He wondered how he had ever believed that he was meant to be with Sarah – how he had ever managed to deceive himself into thinking he was happy. He guessed none of that mattered now. As he looked sideways at Jeremy, pulling a silly face as he bit into his own sandwich, he realized that he was actually sort of hoping Sarah did tell the media about their relationship. Maybe if she didn't, they could go and do an interview of their own volition.

After all – who wouldn't be proud of a man as kind, patient and forgiving as this?

Chapter 13

Maybe in wishing that Sarah would go to the media, Dan had spoken too soon. At the time, it had seemed like she could do no damage – which he and Jeremy could stand up to any kind of smear she attempted to make on them. The gay rights movement in this country was snowballing, after all; equal marriage had finally been voted in, and it continued to make leaps and bounds forward. It felt like the media would be on their side, rather than hers.

Unfortunately, Dan had sorely underestimated the way his ex could re-frame things against him.

It was a few weeks later on a cool spring morning that they woke up to the mayhem. Predictably enough, it was Dan's phone that started making noise first. Texts, tweets, calls and all manner of other alerts started vibrating and flashing his phone on the nightstand so hard that he could no longer sleep through it. Jeremy grunted as he felt Dan move, and Dan felt a little mean for disturbing him – but then he saw the preview of one of his messages on the screen, and a few seconds later Jeremy's phone started blowing up too.

"Shit," he said, nudging Jeremy with his elbow, and rubbing the sleep out of his eyes with his spare hand. "Wake up. Baby; get up."

"What? What is it?"

"We fucked up. That's what. We pissed her off."

Dan's eyes could barely move fast enough for the amount of alerts that were coming through, but he didn't have to read each one individually in order to understand. He could see shocking headlines, incriminating allegations, and one repeated picture, over and over again – Sarah feigning tears in a TV studio.

She had done an interview about him and Jeremy.

Hockey Pregnancy Hell: My Cheating Gay Husband.

"Calm down," Jeremy told him, still waking up, and reached for his phone. "Who did we piss off? What's the matter?"

"Sarah," he clarified, realizing he hadn't exactly been specific. "She's gone to the media like we guessed, but... she's claiming to be pregnant. Claiming I just disappeared on her. I mean... she's crying in this interview, on camera."

"...Shit."

There could be no overstating how bad this was for Dan and his career. It was all bullshit, of course. Dan was pretty sure Sarah wasn't pregnant. He'd be lying if he said he paid enough attention to her when they were married, but he had at least noticed some things – like the fact that she had asked him to pick up some tampons for her only a week before their argument, and the fact they hadn't fucked in months. She couldn't possibly be pregnant.

Could she?

Unless...

"It's his baby, isn't it?" said Jeremy, voicing the thought that Dan had just had. "She's fallen pregnant with Devon, and now she's going to use that kid too... well. Do this."

"She'll be after money, too," Dan pointed out. "She'll use this for leverage through the divorce. She was already going to bleed me dry, and now this, and... fuck!"

Jeremy rubbed his shoulder absently, still scrolling through his own notifications. There weren't as many industry contacts in his phone, but he still had family and friends awake at this hour – still had people who had seen his name dragged into this, and who wanted to know what the hell was going on. Dan felt terrible. His boyfriend hadn't asked for any of this. Granted, he hadn't either, but... well. He'd married her in the first place. He'd been the one to get her so mad.

"It's going to be alright," Jeremy assured him. "Don't get me wrong. It's going to be messy, and there are going to be people who believe her over you, but... the truth is on your side. If you're honest and open with the media, then they'll back you. In the end, she won't be able to verify any part of her story."

"Won't she?" said Dan, dropping his phone heavily onto the bed. He was done with replying to texts for now; it was getting to be too much. "I feel like she's the kind of person who's going to have all her bases covered."

"With lies," Jeremy clarified. "Let's just go back to square one here. You didn't run off and cheat on her – with a man or a woman. She cheated on you. She left you, then you and I got back together. She wasn't pregnant when she left you. You have teammates who can vouch for the fact that she's been sleeping around for a while. Surely, they're going to be on your side here?"

Dan shook his head, his mind in pieces. "I'd like to think so, but... god. Who the hell knows? She might have gotten to them already."

"Relax," Jeremy told him, still rubbing his arm soothingly – but paying more attention to him than the phone now. "This isn't the Bourne Identity. Nobody's getting to anybody. If there's blackmail or bribing involved, it'd only get worse for her. The truth is on your side, baby. We'll get it out there. If anything, this is just going to catapult your career."

"How could it?"

"Well," said Jeremy, carding a hand through his hair. "Being one of the first out and proud professional sportsmen in the US is a good thing, you know? You're a trailblazer now. Sure, she pulled you out of the closet – but we were planning to make the announcement ourselves. Your agent has all the plans; they can show them to the press. Trust me. The world is not going to love the woman trying to put you on blast for being who you are. They're going to love you."

Dan hummed, shaking his head, and leaned to give his boyfriend a kiss on the shoulder. "If anything, they're going to love us."

That seemed to be the right thing to say. Jeremy grinned, cuddling up to him. "That's right. So... let's just weather this, okay? It's shitty, but don't panic. It's temporary, and you've still got me on your side no matter what."

Dan only hoped that would be enough. As his phone continued to blow up even now that it was on silent, he tried to believe in everything that Jeremy said – but until their side of the story was actually out there and well-received, he knew that he couldn't be sure.

Chapter 14

The day seemed to stretch on for at least twice as long as usual. No matter how many calls Dan answered, or how many emails he responded to, the requests for comment just kept pouring in. Why his team's management couldn't deal with this, he wasn't sure – but for now, it didn't matter. All this bullshit was landing right in his lap, and he was going to have to do something about it.

"Yes, of course, we're denying it," he said, halfway through another tense phone call with the team's legal department. "It's not true."

"You're not gay?" the stern-sounding voice asked.

Dan paused, scrubbing at his face with his hand. Boy, had he ever underestimated his ex. He should have known she'd be able to screw him over like this – that she'd know to tell a few lies and a few truths so he couldn't cleanly deny everything. He was forced to sift through the bullshit and forced to appear a little bit guilty somehow, even if he hadn't done a single thing wrong.

Fuck her.

"I am gay," he clarified. "But I didn't cheat on her. And if she is pregnant, then it's not with my child."

He rolled his eyes at Jeremy, who was making his way over to rub his back. Things had been crazy all day, but at least Dan was lucky enough to have his boyfriend's company. There was no training going on at the school today, so there was nothing to pull him away – not even the errands Jeremy had been wanting to run. He had always been self-sacrificing that way. It made Dan feel even guiltier that he had ever abandoned the guy. Clearly, he had walked away from one of the best people in his life. No matter the justification he thought he had for that at the time, it was maddening.

Well – he couldn't change the past now. All he could do was treat Jeremy better from now on, and he certainly did intend to do that. The man wasn't going to get out of his sight again easily.

The stern-sounding voice hummed. "Right..." Dan could hear the sound of a pencil on paper. "Okay. You will both need to be flexible in terms of, ah... making appearances, attending interviews. That will all be necessary if we want to fix this. She's getting her story distributed very widely, so we need to combat that."

"That's fine with us," said Dan, glancing at Jeremy, who confirmed with a nod, still massaging at Dan's shoulders. "We'll go wherever you need us."

"To confirm," said the voice, "everything you have told me is, without a doubt, the honest truth? She cannot be pregnant with your child, and you never cheated on her – either with Jeremy or with another person, male or female?"

Dan gritted his teeth, trying to stay calm. It wasn't that they disbelieved him, he told himself. This was simply protocol. "Yes, absolutely, that's all true."

"And the reason you know she cannot be pregnant...?"

He sighed. "That's not obvious?"

"There are a number of different reasons," the voice replied. "Your word that you haven't slept together in a long time is one thing. Your medical inability to conceive would be quite another."

"Well, sorry about that," said Dan, beginning to feel irritated. "You've only got my word."

"It's just vital that we have all the information we need to build your case for you," said the voice, sounding largely unperturbed by Dan's frustration. "And if there are any surprises that we should know about, it's helpful for us to be able to prepare for them in advance."

"Like what?"

"Old lovers coming to testify against you."

Dan's grip clenched around the phone. "I told you. There aren't any. I was completely faithful to her. I didn't even meet Jeremy again until after she left me."

"We're just covering our bases, Daniel. It's for the best for both you and for us."

"Great," he said, only very poorly covering up his irritation now. "Well, thanks. If you could start booking opportunities for us to fix this, we'd both be grateful."

"We'll be in touch."

Just as he hung up, the phone started ringing again – but he was way too stressed to answer it. He groaned, tossing his cell aside onto the soft surface of the couch, and turned to face Jeremy instead. "This is total bullshit. I'm pretty sure even the team legal department doesn't believe me."

Jeremy wrapped his arms around his shoulders, already working at calming him down. "That's their job," he insisted, voice soft. "Not to believe you, I mean. They have to be prepared for whatever happens; the media will be giving you the exact same scrutiny. They need to be sure you have answers for when those questions come."

"If they phrased it like that, I wouldn't mind," Dan insisted. "They just act like I've done something wrong, or like they're not on my side. It feels like the entire world is after us right now. Don't you feel like that?"

Jeremy sighed, leaning against his shoulder and pressing a soft kiss to his neck. "Not the whole world, baby. Just the ones she's managed to poison. We'll get there; they'll come around. It's very, very temporary."

"Doesn't feel like it."

"I know," he assured him. "But just a little patience and effort, and we'll clear this all up. You'll see."

Unfortunately, Dan didn't share his optimism. Though Jeremy's explanation for the team member's tough questioning made sense, Dan somehow suspected that their disbelief ran deeper than that. If he was right, then they were in serious trouble. Without the legal team and the PR team on their side, Dan and Jeremy would be up shit creek without a paddle, forced to find their own platforms from which to tell the truth, and with no advice whatsoever on how to go about it.

The only comfort was the man in his arms. No matter what happened, Jeremy seemed to be able to stay calm – and in a storm like this, that kind of rock of support was exactly what Dan needed.

Chapter 15

The first chance they had to address the scandal was on a national sports news channel – with approximately two hours' notice. Dan had given live interviews before, and wasn't too nervous about the concept of that; he just wanted to make sure he gave the best response possible to Sarah's awful allegations.

About twenty minutes before they were due to go on air, however, he noticed that there was a strange tension in Jeremy's shoulders – something he had never previously seen.

"Hey," he said, turning to him the moment he realized. "Are you okay?"

Jeremy smiled, a little sheepish. "Oh, you know. Panic. Mild nausea. The usual."

"Seriously?" Dan said, feeling terrible that he hadn't yet noticed. He turned in his seat to face Jeremy better, eyes flicking over his face. Sure enough, Jeremy was paler than usual. Had Dan really been so absorbed in his preparations that he hadn't noticed his boyfriend struggling like this? He really needed to get used to paying him more attention. "Jeremy, I'm so sorry. You should have said something."

"You were busy," Jeremy insisted. "We both were, getting up to speed with the latest things she said, so... I figured that was more important than a little stage fright."

"No way," Dan said. "Not at all. Listen – you don't even have to speak if you don't want to. I can speak for both of us."

At this, Jeremy did seem to perk up a little. "You're sure?"

"Baby, of course," he said, still feeling rushes of guilt in his chest. "I've done this a thousand times. I'm good at interviews. The most you'll need to do is 'yes' or 'no', and I can elaborate from there."

"They won't try to ask me anything...?"

"If they do, I can just take over. Honestly, Jeremy. It's going to be fine. We've got this. I just feel so awful; if I'd have known, I would never have brought you on air with me. They could have just shown a photo or something..."

"No," Jeremy insisted. "I need to be here in front of the camera. I know that much – but I won't lie. It would feel better if I didn't have to talk."

"Okay," Dan confirmed, nodding and squeezing his shoulder. "That's settled, then. I'll talk. Don't panic; just breathe it out. Here – let's get some water..."

This entire situation was horrible, of course; Dan didn't mind giving interviews, but giving one to deny his ex's gross lies wasn't exactly his idea of fun. For Jeremy to be so afraid of it, however, added yet another element of unpleasantness to it. He had been so calm up until now that Dan had just assumed he was okay with everything they had to do.

He needed to stop making assumptions. Assuming that Sarah couldn't do any damage was what had gotten them into this whole mess.

"Dan and Jeremy?" said a frazzled-looking runner, poking his microphoned-up head into their waiting room. "Hi. We've got ten minutes until you're on. Would you mind heading up with me now?"

Dan looked to Jeremy, concerned. "Is that okay? Are you ready?"

Though he still seemed pale and nervous, Jeremy at least looked a little better than he had when Dan first noticed him. "I'll have to be, I guess. Let's go."

Perhaps noticing his nervousness too, the runner looked back at Jeremy as he led them out of the room. "There's still a little while left before you're on. We've got water set out for you there, and... uh. Don't mention it, but I'm pretty sure my producer would be able to get you a lorazepam if you think that would help...?"

"No, thank you," Jeremy assured him, sharing a quick glance with Dan. Not that he didn't like the idea of something helping his boyfriend to calm down, but Dan could see the headline in his mind's eye now – Hockey Scandal Boyfriend Takes Illegal Prescription Drugs at Whistle Media. It was simply best not to give them the ammunition. Besides, Jeremy's anxiety about being interviewed was perfectly normal. Unlike Dan, he wasn't used to being in the public eye, and it was nothing he had been asked to do before; unlike Sarah, he wasn't a natural born manipulator, capable of telling any untruth to any listening ear.

Who could possibly expect him to be media-ready out of the blue?

"Alright," said the runner, gesturing towards a pair of stiff-looking armchairs in front of a camera set-up. "The host will join you in here after the next advertisement break. If you need anything until then, my name is Henry. Good luck."

He started heading away, then paused and turned back.

"For the record?" he said, slightly halting and shy. "I don't believe a word she said. I'm a drama queen myself. I know an attention whore when I see one. Knock them dead."

Jeremy grinned at Dan as the runner turned on his heel and went back to work, seeming to relax slightly into the stiff chair. "See? It's not the whole world like I said. Some people are still on our side."

"Let's just hope there are more Henry's in the world than there are Sarah's."

The wait for the host to appear was tense for Dan despite his experience, so he couldn't imagine what Jeremy was feeling. He reached across to squeeze his hand, slightly comforted by Jeremy's determined smile and steeled himself for the scrutiny he was about to endure.

He realized that his father might be watching, but he kind of had to live with that. There was no going back now. His parents would find out about this one way or another; they may as well see the truth from their own son.

When the host arrived, it was with a slight jog. Apparently, this was a studio they didn't use very often, and he had struggled to make it over from the other set – but he greeted them both with a formal handshake, gathering himself together as he sat in the chair opposite them.

"You boys ready for this?" he asked, voice a little gruffer than Dan had been hoping. "We've got some pretty tough questions for both of you."

"Actually," said Dan, "it's me that will be answering the questions. Jeremy is here for support, but he's not comfortable with the live interview."

The host drew his eyes over Jeremy, unkind and judgmental. "I see." It was then that Dan knew this would be a difficult and turbulent couple of minutes – but that didn't change a thing. He was still going to try his best, and the truth was still on their side. No matter what this asshole said, he couldn't change either of those things.

"On in thirty seconds, Bryan," said Henry the runner, flustered as he skipped from spot to spot behind the cameras and the lights. The studio seemed understaffed today – and where was the actual producer? Was he still in the main studio? Was this interview not deemed important enough for his presence? "Twenty."

"Let's keep this formal," said the host Bryan, adjusting his hair in the reflection of the table. "We're here to discuss rumors, not make friends. I'm not taking either side. I don't want any counter-slander."

Dan felt Jeremy's hand rest on his back, and he knew somehow that this was a sign to stay steady and calm. He doesn't matter. Don't let him get a rise out of you.

If that was what Jeremy meant, then Dan knew he was right. If they let this host get under their skin in any way, then they'd be playing right into Sarah's hands – and his career might just disappear before their eyes, as well as their reputations nationwide.

"Ten seconds. Nine. Eight. Seven..."

Dan turned the runner out as he focused his mind on the interview, and on the truth. Before he knew it, the red light was on, and Bryan no longer looked like a grumpy diva of a host. Instead, he wore a smile like a second-hand car salesman.

"Welcome back to In Sport Today. As promised, we're now joined by Dan Carter and Jeremy Green. Now – Dan. In the age of social media, instant gratification, Twitter... all that immediate delivery of the news. How has today been for you? It seems like these allegations just popped up overnight."

"That's exactly right, Bryan," he agreed. "We woke up this morning and everything had just exploded. It's the first time either of us had heard any of the stories being told about me; none of this is anything I'm familiar with."

"But you did have a relationship with this woman?"

"That's correct," said Dan. "We were married, up until quite recently – then..."

The story tumbled out with ease. There was nothing for him to hide, and nothing to withhold; as such, he didn't need to edit himself, or watch out for any pitfalls. In fact, he actually kind of enjoyed it. Usually, when he gave interviews he was defending something, selling something or trying to project confidence for the season; now, all that he needed to focus on was the truth.

Frankly, the truth was a good story. His life had changed for the better over the past few weeks, and he was pleased with the place those changes had brought him to. With Jeremy by his side, he was better-equipped to enjoy his life and his career than he had been in several years.

Unfortunately, Bryan didn't seem to feel the same way – not even with that salesman smile on his shiny, Botox-riddled face.

"Now, I have to ask," he said, having just heard the full story, "you married this woman, and she was under the understanding that you were heterosexual. That you had no attraction to men."

"We never discussed it," Dan pointed out. "But no, I don't think she had any reason to believe I was interested in men."

Bryan lifted a hand, encouraging Dan to elaborate, and added, "That isn't considered some kind of lie? Withholding that kind of information from your spouse?"

"Well… not really, no," said Dan, shuffling in his chair. This wasn't a line of questioning he had been expecting, and it certainly wasn't one he liked. "At the time I thought that my relationship with Jeremy had been… you know some kind of fluke. Experimentation that I had gotten out of my system, I thought that I was straight. My fondness for her was genuine, and I really believed that I loved her."

"You don't think that's information she deserves to know about the man she's marrying?"

Had his team not thought to check whether this man Bryan was anti-gay, to begin with? Recalling Jeremy's silent advice not to get riled up, Dan forced himself to stay calm. "I don't think so, no. It was in my past – a part of my past that I had struggled with, and didn't like to think about. I wanted to be with her, and she wanted to be with me. I didn't… ask for her full sexual history, and she didn't ask for mine. I don't feel that should be a concern."

"You wouldn't have minded if she had – say, been with a woman before you?"

Dan couldn't help but show his incredulity, shaking his head with a short laugh. "Well – no, of course not, all that matters is what happens while we're together. If Jeremy had been with a woman before me, then… that's fine. If he were to leave me now and date a woman – please don't," he said, turning briefly to Jeremy with a smile, "then that's fine too."

"I think there could be an argument made that she had a right to know that there was a risk you'd fall for a man and leave her," said Bryan, holding his hands up innocently. "That's all I'm saying."

"I believe it's about whether you cheat or not," Dan said, trying to pull the interview back on track. "Not who you would choose to cheat with. And I never cheated on Sarah."

"Unfortunately, it's your word against hers."

"I'm sure my teammates could corroborate," said Dan. "If you asked them, she left me the day before our last friendly match; I didn't speak about it, but Zack Kazamakis could testify to the fact that I was down; he took the time to check up on me. After the match, I went to a party where I was reunited with Jeremy. The first time I'd seen him since college."

"There weren't any other men in the time you were together?"

"Not at all," said Dan, forcing himself to stay calm. Do not give this asshole the reaction he wants. Don't play into his hands – or Sarah's. "I was completely faithful to Sarah for the entire time we were together."

Jeremy cleared his throat, drawing Dan's eye. Surprisingly, he then shuffled forward to speak. His voice was quiet and mousy, but the fact that he had drawn up his courage and was speaking at all filled Dan up with pride. "Actually, as far as I'm concerned, it's Sarah who was unfaithful to Dan. There's a baseball player – is it Devon?"

"Devon is her current partner," confirmed the host. "A professional batsman for the Mariners, if that is who you mean."

"That's right," said Jeremy, voice faltering only slightly, but he held his ground. "I think there's some reason to believe that relationship has been going on for much longer than she has stated."

"What; you're... accusing her of being the cheater, now?"

Bryan didn't seem best pleased with this – but of course, Jeremy was right. Dan nodded, patting Jeremy's hand with his.

"Listen – as far as I'm concerned, my relationship with Sarah is over. It's finished; we'll be going through divorce proceedings over the next few months. Had she not brought the conversation to the public sphere, I'd consider that our business. As things stand... well. She's accusing me of being the one to corrupt our marriage, and that's just not true. In fact, she moved directly out of our house into Devon's; I'm sure there's some way to prove that."

"And you're suggesting that this pregnancy... this would be the result of her relationship with Devon Adams, not her marriage to you?"

"That's correct," said Dan, nodding slowly. "Not to put too fine a point on it on your family-friendly show, Bryan, but... there is no physical possibility that Sarah is pregnant with my child."

"Alright," said Bryan, clearly dissatisfied with his answer, but checking the clock that was on the camera. They were out of time. "Well – thank you gentlemen for coming on our show today. I'm not sure we got to the bottom of this, but I appreciate your time; I'm sure our viewers do too."

"You're very welcome," said Dan, squeezing Jeremy's hand as he felt it slide into his. His ordeal was nearly over – but as Bryan told his viewers they'd be back after the break and stood immediately up from the chair once the red light had gone out, ignoring the two of them entirely, Dan knew that the wider ordeal was about to begin. This had not been a friendly interview, and if it set the tone for the rest of the media coverage, then Dan really didn't know whether this would go the way they wanted it to.

Maybe his father had been right after all. Maybe the world of sport had no interest in accommodating gay athletes.

Chapter 16

As they returned home that night, both Dan and Jeremy felt drained. Even just climbing into their car outside the studio had been difficult, as they were surrounded by reporters trying to get comments. It was hard to deny you were at a studio, after all, if you had just been shown giving a live interview there. All the same, as they finally shut the door of Jeremy's apartment behind them, they were at last able to relax into their own company again.

"We're good?"

"I think so," Jeremy replied, hanging off his coat. He still looked pale, but otherwise, he seemed to have recovered quickly from his TV appearance. "I don't know exactly how that will be perceived, but... he was coming for you a little too strong, I thought. It's not the kind of treatment you'd get on a gay-friendly network."

"Maybe that will work in our favor, at least," sighed Dan, heading through to the kitchen. "Like you said, it's not good to sit through it, but then I guess people will at least understand what kind of bias we're dealing with. You want a beer?"

"Please," Jeremy answered, following him through. "Though – you know, this is actually my house, my beer."

Dan looked up, momentarily concerned that he'd overstepped, but then caught sight of the grin on Jeremy's face "Man, you can't do that to me," he said, handing over a beer with the lid already popped off. "You'll scare the life out of me like that."

"I know," said Jeremy, pecking him on the cheek. "It's kind of sweet, though, actually. It's like we've stepped right back into the place we were at college, you know? Like we never left."

"I like that too," Dan assured him, leaning against the counter. "Kind of helps with the guilt."

"You don't honestly still feel bad about it?" Jeremy asked, tilting his head at Dan. "Oh, come on; I told you. Things are better now. I understand why it happened, and... here we are again. It's okay."

"I know," said Dan, "and I believe you. I just know you deserve better than the way I treated you, and I know I can't ever go back and fix it. It's frustrating – that's all."

"Well, just don't beat yourself up about it in public," Jeremy told him. "Don't give them another angle to attack us from, whatever you do."

Dan laughed quietly, knowing that he was right. If Sarah could make it look like he was bad for Jeremy as well as bad for her, then they'd really never recover from this mess. "Right, I'll remember not to cry about it – next interview."

"God," said Jeremy, tilting his head back. "I can't believe we have to do that all over again."

"It'll be easier the second time," Dan assured him – though he wasn't entirely sure that was true, he still wanted to offer the comfort. "Besides, you managed to speak. I was really proud of that."

"I... still really don't know how that happened," Jeremy admitted. "It just sort of came out. I could tell you weren't going to point it out – especially after he told you he didn't want any counter-drama – but... it needed to be out there."

"Defending me, huh?"

They locked eyes across the kitchen, finally looking down into their beer bottles. It was crazy to stand here in Jeremy's kitchen now, feeling that same connection they had formed so many years ago. No matter what was going on outside their front door in the media world, and no matter how turbulent their lives got, they could still stand here with each other's company.

He may have married Sarah, but he had never felt this close to her. Though he would have allowed her to lean on him, he had never felt able to lean on her like this.

"Hey," he said, after a few beats. "I'm really glad we're here. Even with all of this."

Jeremy smiled at him, crossing over the small kitchen to stand beside him and lean in for a soft, quick kiss. "Me too." But when he pulled away, the magnetism between them remained too strong; he only moved away a couple of inches, both their eyes roving over each other, before their lips met again, kissing strong and deep as Dan wrapped his arms around Jeremy's waist, pulling him closer in.

"I missed this."

Jeremy's hands pressed up firm and fond against his chest, fingers circling lightly over his shirt; encouraged, Dan's hands snaked down from his waist to smooth over his ass. It was becoming clear pretty quickly that this wasn't going to remain just a soft, romantic kiss. Already, he could feel Jeremy's hips rocking into his, and the feeling of his cock beginning to grow hard against Dan's thigh.

"Maybe we should move somewhere else," he suggested, voice already low and raw with desire – but Jeremy shook his head, nose brushing playfully against Dan's.

"Here is good," he insisted, interrupting his own words with a light kiss. "Right here."

"Yeah?"

Clearly, Jeremy had a plan; he peeled himself out of Dan's grip, shuffling back up against the counter. "Lift me up."

Dan was powerless to do anything but obey – and frankly, he didn't want to do anything but obey. Jeremy was so handsome, and it was so hot to hear him give orders like this, even if only playfully. As such, he did as he was told, lifting Jeremy up to plant him firmly on the counter.

"Good," said Jeremy, arms wrapping around his neck as he leaned in to give him one more messy, eager kiss. After that, there was no need for words; his hands stroked through the back of Dan's hair, and Dan already knew what he was going to do. Sure enough, as the kiss broke, Jeremy pushed gently at the back of Dan's head – and he curled willingly over his partner's lap to obey.

Dan pressed a line of eager kisses up his boyfriend's thigh. Even through his denim jeans, Jeremy clearly enjoyed the sensation of Dan's kisses, already humming with pleasure. No doubt about it, their sexual chemistry had blown up in college, and then never left them since. Already, Dan could feel himself getting hard at the mere thought of Jeremy's thick, handsome cock, though all he could see of it was its outline in his jeans.

"You're so beautiful," he murmured against his leg, unsure if Jeremy could even hear him, but inclined to say it anyway. After all, it was true. Looking up at his boyfriend from this angle, he saw such handsome bone structure and intense eyes that set fire to every inch of him. He could swallow him whole – and he intended to, of course.

Jeremy's hands carded through his hair, rough and keen, as Dan began unbuttoning his boyfriend's jeans and working them down his legs. Jeremy lifted his ass, eager to help undress, and soon he was liberated of the tight denim fabric. Beneath them was a pair of bright blue boxer-briefs, straining to contain Jeremy's erection.

"Yeah?" Dan teased, eyes flicking up to meet Jeremy's. "You want me?"

"God, yeah."

Dan wasted no time in pulling down his underwear, desperate to reach the bare skin beneath – and sure enough, the payoff was perfect. He groaned as he sank down to press dozens of kisses against the bare skin of his thigh, eyes fixed on the dark spring of Jeremy's cock between his legs. He took him in his hand first for a few broad strokes, licking his lips at the sight of him – and then, glancing up to waste another second and to make Jeremy's eyes beg a little longer, he leaned closer.

"Let's see if I remember how to do this," he said playfully as ever with his partner and took him eagerly into his mouth.

It was hard to take all of Jeremy's cock at once. Not only was he long, but he was thick; even so, Dan couldn't wait to swallow him whole, one hand spare to fondle feather-light at his balls as he worked up and down Jeremy's cock. It had been so long since he had done this that he'd forgotten how much pleasure it gave him, his own dick straining against the restraint of his pants as he pressed up against the counter for a little friction. Soon, he promised himself. But he had to focus on Jeremy first.

He could feel Jeremy's hand tightening in his hair, trying to ignore the uncomfortable sensation of slightly gagging on the length of him; pulling back for a moment to breathe, he pressed a few kisses along his shaft, drinking in the sounds of Jeremy's moans and pants.

"Yeah?" he asked mouth free for a few moments. "Is it good? You like that?"

"So good," Jeremy assured him, eyes falling open for a few moments to grin weakly at him. "God, please. Dan…"

Knowing he was doing such a good job of pleasing his partner only spurred him on to finish, and he finally gave himself permission to reach down with a spare hand and free his own cock, already sucking hard at Jeremy again. He could feel the tension working up in Jeremy's legs, and the way his feet had begun to curl around the backs of Dan's legs; he knew that he was close to finishing, and tugged at himself fast and hard in the hopes that they would time up together.

"So close," Jeremy warned him – but Dan had no intention of pulling away. He wanted every last drop, and he wanted Jeremy to see him take it.

Soon enough, he got his wish. Thrusting hard into his own hand, he heard something in Jeremy snap; it gave a second's warning before he came heavily into Dan's mouth, his fingers tangled tight in Dan's hair and ass sliding forwards on the counter, bucking into the pleasure with little concept of where he was remaining.

This was how he liked to fuck his partner – so good that he could barely keep track of himself. He liked to unpick Jeremy's stitches with pleasure, and then put him back together again. As he tipped himself over the edge, coming into his own hand with a quiet grunt, Dan felt he'd done a good job of that unpicking-and-pleasure today.

At least, he had to judge by the soppy, closed-eyes grin on Jeremy's face.

"How're you doing up there, handsome?" he teased, kissing his knee as he reached for a paper towel to wipe off his hand. "You doing okay?"

"I am... so much better than okay."

Dan helped him down off the counter, holding an arm around his waist in case he was unsteady. Jeremy leaned forward to reward him with a fond, long kiss.

"Like riding a bike, huh?" he teased. "You never forget how to suck dick."

"We'd better not tell the media," Dan joked right back, leading Jeremy through to flop down on the couch, spent and satisfied. "They'll probably want to know who I practiced on all those years."

"Babe, I want to know who you practiced on. I'm really jealous."

Dan opened his mouth to insist that he hadn't, only catching Jeremy's sly grin at the last minute. "God, you're a torment. Stop teasing me. You'll give me gray hairs."

"You'd look pretty dignified that way, I think," said Jeremy, ruffling through his hair a lot softer now that he wasn't in the throes of passion. "All salt and pepper."

"Not for a few more years, I hope," Dan complained. Gray hair didn't start until a lot later in his family's genetic history, so he figured he was safe – but everybody aged differently. There was no way of telling. Somehow, however, he actually believed what Jeremy said. It both frightened and excited him that he could really picture himself growing old with Jeremy like this, play-fighting and fucking and teasing each other to retirement.

Jeremy sighed, flopping down even more against Dan's chest. "Can I say something stupid?"

Feeling the same thing well up in him, Dan bent to kiss the top of his head. "Go ahead."

"I love you."

Even though he had seen it coming, it still took Dan's breath away to hear him say that. He pressed another kiss to his forehead, trying to stay cool, and then leaned his head against Jeremy's. He wasn't at all afraid or reluctant to say it. Frankly, he didn't think he'd ever been this certain before – not about anything in his entire life. "I love you, too."

Get a load of that, Bryan from Whistle Media.

Chapter 17

As it turned out, their interview on In Sport Today was better received than they expected. As Jeremy had hoped – and predicted – there were many people who identified the bias in the host's line of questioning, and who rallied to both Dan's and Jeremy's defense. Others seemed not to be sure; as it was a live interview, In Sport Today had clearly not had time to follow up on the claims that Dan had made about what his teammates would and would not corroborate, and that meant that for some people, it wasn't valid proof.

Even so, it was a step in the right direction, and today Dan didn't feel so afraid to step out of the house – even holding Jeremy's hand.

"That's big, for you," Jeremy pointed out, once they had climbed into the car. "Holding my hand out in public."

"It was only on our street."

"Still," said Jeremy, leaning across the car to peck his cheek. "I liked it."

They were on their way out to a far more gay-friendly venue today – an interview with PinkNews. Initially, the team's legal department had not seemed convinced that this was a big enough or mainstream enough source to host their argument, but it had been this site which led the charge against Bryan's comments yesterday, and so the department had relented.

"I'm actually not so afraid of this one," Jeremy said, once they finally arrived at the right studio. "I don't know whether that's because I know they're on our side, or because I already did it yesterday, but... progress, right?"

"Absolutely," said Dan. He himself had predicted that this interview wouldn't scare Jeremy as much because it wasn't live, but he didn't want to detract from Jeremy's progress. He was really proud of how Jeremy was facing his fears for this, and grateful for it too. "You're pretty awesome."

Jeremy wrinkled his nose. "I figure somebody awesome wouldn't be so scared in the first place."

"How is that awesome?" Dan argued playfully, holding the door open for Jeremy as he climbed out. "Doing things that come easily to you is just... doing things."

"I suppose so."

"It's like people always say. Bravery isn't about not being scared; it's about being scared and doing it anyway. Right?"

"Stop it," said Jeremy, leading him into the building. "You'll give me an ego."

Dan grinned, feeling good vibes for the day – and sure enough, he was right. Their interview with PinkNews was thorough, featuring actual evidence from all the sources that Dan had mentioned in the previous interview. At least some of his teammates had come through for him, even if a couple of them seemed to be keeping silent on the matter; that much, he had expected. He'd heard the homophobic humor in the changing rooms from a few of them and certainly hadn't anticipated full support. A statement from Zack helped out, however, and he made a mental note to thank the guy later. He had always been a better friend than Dan really gave him credit for.

In fact, it had almost gone perfectly – right up until the end of the interview, when an intern awkwardly interrupted.

"I'm sorry," she said, stopping the interviewer Marcie as she was noting something down. "But I'm supposed to ask you all to look at Twitter. Sarah has released some more information. Sorry to interrupt."

With that, she dashed out – and this was the moment that both Dan and Jeremy knew that something pretty bad had been added to the mix.

Marcie's eyes widened as she glanced at her phone. "Ah – yeah," she said. "You're going to want to look at that. We've got abuse allegations."

Dan was already reading some choice quotes from Sarah's statement. *Daniel is a very good liar and a manipulator. I'm not* surprised that he's winning people over. He won me over for long enough, but I'm tired of protecting him. He was abusive towards me for years. I wasn't going to turn this into anything that could get him into trouble, but... the cycle should end now. I didn't leave his home to run into Devon's arms; I left to live with Devon because my home with Daniel was unsafe for me and our unborn child.

When he looked up, both Jeremy and Marcie were looking at him with slack jaws.

"Well, it sure isn't true," he pointed out after a long pause, flabbergasted that she would stoop this low. "I never, ever touched her. Not like that."

"What about the supporting statement?" asked Marcie, concerned. "Did you read that?" At the confused look on his face, she handed him her phone.

"...Oh, fuck this guy."

There on the screen, Dan saw a photograph of the guy at the party who he had almost gotten into a fight with – the guy who had bumped into him and wanted to cause trouble. I was at an event with Daniel Carter the evening after this supposed breakup he's talking about. He claims he was down and upset, but the way I remember it, he was aggressive and violent. I narrowly avoided coming to blows with him. It wouldn't shock me at all if Sarah's allegations were true.

"This is just some jerk," he insisted, passing the phone to Jeremy. "You recognize this asshole, right, Jeremy? He was crazy drunk – just falling around all over. He knocked into me and was trying to be a wise-ass. I told him to go home before he got himself into trouble. You can ask my teammates about him too – call Zack again. He'll tell you."

"You know," said Jeremy, "I think you have something else you can point towards, too."

Both Dan and Marcie turned to him, confused.

"Dan, do you remember that day in the grocery store? You bumped into Sarah and Devon in there. They must have CCTV, or...?"

Dan blinked for a few moments, and then the recognition hit him. "Oh, wow. Yeah, you're right. Call the SuperMart near my address. I think it's on Spring Street? This would have been, uh…"

"Thursday," supplied Jeremy.

"The Thursday after she left, Devon assaulted me; they were trying to encourage me to fight him, I guess, but I didn't rise to it, just walked away. Wouldn't do that if I was a violent character, surely?"

Marcie nodded eagerly, writing all of this information down. "Okay, good. That's good. We'll definitely look into getting hold of that footage." She was great; Dan could really tell that she was on their side. She was acting almost like a lawyer, helping them to patch their story together with evidence, and poke holes in Sarah's claims.

Actually, shouldn't this be what his PR team was doing?

"I know she's trying to get at you," Marcie said, "and I know it must be pretty rough to be you guys right now, but honestly – the tide is really turning in your favor. You can tell she's panicking right now. I mean… abuse allegations? She knows she's been proven wrong, and she clearly didn't expect you to fight back, so she had no idea what she was getting herself into. You've got this."

"Really?"

"Nonsense like that?" she said, wrinkling her nose up. "That's Sarah in death throes, I assure you. She's lashing out with any old shit she can land on; it's so easy to disprove. You just keep doing what you're doing. Your ex is going to talk herself into a corner she can't back out of any day now."

Chapter 18

With the media beginning to turn in their favor, Dan and Jeremy no longer felt so much pressure to hide away at home – though admittedly, they had stuck to Jeremy's place instead of Dan's. They dreaded to think what they'd find at that place right now, and besides, they wanted each other's company as much as they wanted anything else. Soon enough, they hoped they would be able to go out and date again. Running out to the grocery store was one thing, but dates were another animal. Right now, for example, things were way too heated for them to go to a restaurant. It was just too intense an environment.

"Still," said Jeremy, lifting the last bag of groceries out of the car. "I guess we're saving a lot of money, and... it's probably healthier, right?"

"Screw healthy," said Dan. "I'm in the off-season. I want steak."

"I can do that."

It still astounded Dan how their banter was so easy after all these years. He guessed he owed a lot to Jeremy for that – for being able to overcome the hurt and heartache that Dan had caused him. A more bitter or fearful person might have never been able to forgive him. Granted, Jeremy had asked to put some distance between them at first, but he had quickly come around. Now, things felt like they couldn't be better.

Well, between the two of them, at least. The world out there still had some thinking to do.

He pressed a kiss behind his ear as they headed into the house. "You know," he said. "You make me feel very lucky."

Jeremy grinned back at him. "It's just a steak."

"Just a steak? There's no such thing."

They chattered their way through putting their food away, easy in each other's company; when the doorbell rang, it didn't seem like a big deal. They felt relaxed and happy – so when they opened the door to Devon Adams's unhappy face, it felt like a slap to theirs.

"We're going to need to talk," he said. He didn't wait to be invited in; he just barged straight past Jeremy into the hallway. That alone got a rise out of Dan, squaring up to him despite Jeremy's quiet pleas for him to calm down.

"It's fine," Jeremy assured him, voice low. "We'll talk. It's okay. Calm down."

"You knock into him again and you'll wish you hadn't," Dan warned him with a pointed finger. "I'm not joking."

"I'm not joking, asshole," Devon barked, practically pacing in the hallway. "You think it's fucking funny to accuse me of assault in an interview? Tell them to check the CCTV?"

Dan narrowed his eyes, incredulous at Devon's anger. "I'm sorry – you're mad at me? You and your girlfriend have been on this smear campaign against me for days now. What; did you expect me to just lie down and take it?"

"You're getting your ass kicked by the media," said Devon. "She deserves that satisfaction. You are playing with shit that could end my fucking career."

"You think this wouldn't end mine?" Dan shot back. "She's accusing me of abuse now; are you fucking stupid? If my team believed that, I'd be out overnight. Luckily for me, it's total bullshit. You actually did come at me in that store."

Devon shook his head, his face an unpleasant grimace. "Take that accusation back. Tell them you lied."

"No," Dan said, almost speechless that Devon would dare to make a request like that – after everything that he and Sarah had done? Was he crazy? "You made your bed, asshole. Now you're just going to have to lie in it."

"Trust me, Carter. This can get way uglier than it already has."

"Try me."

Sparks flew between them in the corridor as Jeremy stood at Dan's shoulder, helpless to defuse it. Dan stared Devon down for a few seconds longer, completely unafraid of what he was threatening. His behavior now only confirmed what the PinkNews interview, Marcie, had said about Sarah's desperation in making up the abuse allegations. Both of them were desperate now. They had not realized how deep they were wading into shit. Well – if Devon didn't want to risk his Marlins career, then he shouldn't have assaulted someone in a public grocery store in the first place.

He certainly shouldn't have gotten with Sarah, but... well. Dan had fallen for her manipulation too in the past, and he guessed that Devon and Sarah was a match made in heaven anyway.

Or hell, depending on how you looked at it.

"I'd actually like you to leave my home now," Jeremy managed, his voice as calm as he could make it. "If not, I'll be forced to call the cops. Pretty sure nobody wants that."

"I'll leave," Devon said, after a pause. "But think about it. I'm serious. This can get much, much worse for you."

"Right," said Dan, watching him head out of the door. Unfortunately for Devon, he didn't believe a word. What else could she possibly accuse him of? Nothing she could prove. Besides, at this point, the more she added on, the less legitimate she made herself look. If she wanted to make some really horrific allegations against him – such as pedophilia or something equally as disgusting and abhorrent – then the media would want to know why she hadn't brought this up in the first place, or taken it to the police while they were together.

Even so, it was kind of alarming that Devon would dare to turn up here and threaten them. Jeremy looked pretty shaken, and once Dan's adrenalin ran down, he figured he would feel pretty shaken too.

"What the hell was that?" he asked, both of them stepping to the window to watch him drive away. "He must be really scared for his career."

"That's not our problem," Jeremy assured him, eyes tracking the car's progress down the road. He seemed to relax then. "It's sad if a career he's passionate about gets spoiled because of this, but... he has nobody to blame but himself. You weren't going to bring the assault to anybody's attention or make a big deal out of it. The only reason we were forced to bring it up was to combat the allegations they made about you."

"Right," said Dan, turning back to face him. "Kind of mind-boggling, I guess they're just a little frayed right now. It's not going the way they wanted."

"Do you think we should call the cops?" Jeremy said. "Let them know he forced his way in here in case he tries to come back?"

"I don't think he'd like it," said Dan, "but I think it'd be a good idea. They want to accuse me of being violent, but... jeez. I can defend myself well enough, but if that guy got angry? Shit. I wouldn't like to see what kind of damage he could really do."

"Me neither."

After the cops, they called Marcie straight away. It seemed only fair to give her the update on the story, as she had been so kind and cooperative with them.

"After all," said Dan. "He only came over here 'cos he's panicking like you said. If they want to lay all their cards on the table and threaten us, then fine. Let's smoke them out."

Chapter 19

Though Dan had been proud to rely on several of his teammates for help in this troubling time, he couldn't honestly say he was looking forward to seeing all of them at practice today. Some of them seemed to be taking Sarah and Devon's side over his, and he imagined that the air would be a little stiff and tense between them for the duration of the practice. He wasn't wrong.

The mood in the changing room was pretty unpleasant when he stepped in, and he could feel the frostiness in the air as some of his teammates shifted away from him. Dan had predicted that might happen, and he had already decided not to rise to it – but that didn't mean it didn't sting a little. Granted, he didn't love every single one of his teammates like a brother, but they still shared a team. They were supposed to be pulling in the same direction, and to have each other's backs.

Lucky that he didn't need them all to have his back, then.

He was certainly pleased when Zack arrived, cutting up the tension with his usual hyperness and bounce. "Hey!" Zack greeted him, bustling up beside him without a care in the world. He seemed impervious to the stiffness the rest of the room felt – like he was waterproof in a flood. "You're still alive, looks like."

"Just about."

"You're keeping up okay?" he said, slapping his shoulder. "No more shitty accusations?"

Dan grinned. Trust Zack to make light of this. Honestly, it was exactly what he needed. "Not yet, but give her a day or so to come up with them, you know? I'm sure she'll be back on form sure enough."

"You better stay on my good side," said Zack, "or I'm going to the media about your hobby of hunting endangered animals."

It was strange laughing into such a quiet room, but Dan forced himself to ignore everybody else and just focus on his friend. "I'll be sure not to piss you off."

"That Marcie Bellum got my testimony, right?"

"She did," Dan confirmed, realizing he was forgetting something. "Thank you so much for that, seriously. It's obviously bullshit to us, but the rest of the world wouldn't be sure without some confirmation, so... you know. We both really appreciate it."

Zack held up his hands. "Hey, no problem, that's what I'm for. But you're going to bring him along to the next meet, right? I'm pretty sure I've never met him."

"Sure," said Dan. "If it looks like people would be okay with that."

For the first time, Zack glanced around the room, acknowledging the others' reactions. When he turned back, it was to roll his eyes and shake his head. "Everybody's fine with it. It's not like you're bringing an axe murderer. He's your boyfriend, a hockey player himself, right?"

"He coaches at a high school now," Dan confirmed. "I met him playing at college."

"So he's got a leg up on all the other partners," Zack muttered playfully out of the corner of his mouth. "He can actually understand what the hell we're talking about."

"Easy," somebody else called from across the changing rooms. "My wife would hand you your ass on a plate for suggesting she doesn't understand hockey."

"And does she?" Zack shot back.

"I mean, sure," their teammate responded, voice thick with sarcasm. "She has to ask who's playing in which colors every now and again when she watches it, but sure."

Dan couldn't be more grateful for Zack's ice-breaking presence. A low rumble of conversation was starting up again, and the attention seemed to be completely off him now – even if it wasn't really the case, that was how it felt. He shot Dan a thankful grin, and Zack elbowed him as he dropped his kit bag down on the bench in front of him.

"You just play as well as you did last season," Zack said. "That's all we need from you."

Unfortunately, though, things didn't remain this positive forever.

Zack may have managed to defuse the tension in the changing rooms, but it wasn't long into practice before things started to get heated again. Dan had endured their distance in the changing room well enough, but it seemed like none of them wanted to partner up with him for drills – that they were reluctant to even to be paired with him for relay running.

Even their coach seemed frustrated. "Okay," he said, arms folded. "This isn't high school, and you aren't all teenage girls. Knock it off."

Apparently, however, this wasn't warning enough, and as they neared the end of the training session, almost everybody seemed frustrated. Even Zack seemed to be getting tired of people ignoring Dan and had started throwing sarcastic comments at those people who were avoiding his eye contact. In the end, coach paired Zack and Dan up permanently.

"Seems like he suits you," said one of their teammates to Zack, as they passed.

That, it seemed, was the final straw.

"Alright, this needs to stop," said Zack, wiping the sweat from his brow. "I was trying to ignore this shit, and I can tell you were too, but... you're going to have to talk to legal about this. This is complete bullshit."

"What are legal going to do?" Dan asked, gesturing at the backs of their teammates as they headed away. Not all of them had been assholes, but there were enough that it was seriously noticeable. "They wouldn't listen to coach either."

"I don't know. They just need to make it clear that this shit isn't going to be tolerated," he said. "I'm serious, man. This could be great for our team, you know? Being one of the leaders for LGBT fans and players, we have the opportunity to change the industry right now if they can all just suck it up."

"I don't think they want to make any change," Dan said, feeling sullen. "I think they like it just the way it is."

Zack nodded, but he wore a lopsided smile. "Well, they'd better buckle up. Pride events are growing every year. It's only a matter of time before homophobia gets weeded out everywhere. It happened with black civil rights, and it's going to happen with this, too."

Dan hesitated, biting back the question in his mouth – but then he caught sight of Zack's half-smirk, and realized he was definitely allowed to ask. "This affects you too?"

"I love women," said Zack. "Trust me. First and foremost, they're my interest – and I'm not trying to hit on you with any of this. But sure; I'd qualify as the letter 'B.'"

"You never said."

Zack shrugged. "Neither did you. I guess we both learned something from this. No reason to shut up about who you are. Right?"

"Right."

"It's only going to cause you shit in the long run."

Dan sighed. "Speaking of which... I'm going to take a jog before I head back. I can't deal with them all shuffling away from me in there right now."

"No worries, man. You probably wouldn't want to be in there while I chew their asses out anyway."

"Yeah?"

Zack swept a hand through his hair, starting to head back in the same direction the others had gone. "They've forgotten we're all playing on the same side. They think they can treat you like that after years of working together? Bullshit. I'm not interested."

Watching Zack take a walk back, Dan realized that he hadn't just gained Jeremy out of this entire situation. He'd gained a closer friend too. Of course, he'd always liked Zack before, but he certainly didn't have any complaints about that.

Chapter 20

If Zack really did chew out their teammates after practice, then Dan didn't hear about it – but he certainly saw the effects. When he got home and called legal, they told him that they were already aware of what had happened today at practice, and they were working on smoothing everything over. They even apologized for the way he'd been treated. Things were a long shot away from the tone they had taken with him when the allegations had first been made.

Was his ordeal finally over? He wasn't getting nearly as many tweets about the situation now, and apparently, he and Jeremy had even been named on a 'Cutest Couples of the Month' list. Surely if the world believed he was a cheater who abandoned his pregnant wife, they wouldn't have made an appearance on that list?

"I'm glad things are finally looking up for us," Jeremy confirmed in bed that night, his arm around Dan and his hand teasing through his hair. "For a minute there in that Whistle Media interview, I thought we were screwed."

"Me, too," Dan admitted against his chest, eyes closed and just enjoying the comfort of being blanketed up after a hard day. "Even just before it started, the way he was speaking to us... I don't know. I think we're going to have to send Marcie Bellum some flowers or something."

"Agreed."

The silence of the room was comforting, and they were about ready to fall asleep – but then the sound of banging on the door interrupted all that peace and quiet.

"Who the hell is that at this time of night?"

Dan's question answered itself a moment later, however, as he heard the familiar voice of Devon Adams roars through their apartment.

"Open this fucking door!"

"Call the cops," Dan told him immediately, flinging the covers off himself to start getting dressed. "I'm going to go make sure the door is secure."

"Be careful," Jeremy told him. It didn't seem like an unnecessary warning. It was obvious from the tone of Devon's voice that he was furious, perhaps because he and Jeremy hadn't obeyed his order to take back their accusations – but Dan had no intention of reneging on the truth.

He made sure the door was deadlocked first, peering through the spyglass at their guest. Sure enough, he looked absolutely livid, and also kind of drunk. "You're not going to get in," he called through the door, his tone clear of anxiety. Sure, it was a shock to hear him banging on the door, but Devon didn't scare him. "We've got CCTV set up out there. You might as well just leave."

"You're a fucking child, Dan Carter," he shouted through the door. Yep – now that Dan was closer, he could hear that Devon was definitely slurring his words. "You want this to be over, and then let's settle it like men."

"I am settling it like a man," Dan drawled. "Upfront, honestly, and without risking my career blowing up in my face. Wish I could say the same for you, but you just had to go and try to be the big man with Sarah."

"You and Sarah have nothing to do with my fucking career," Devon barked. "You've got no fucking right."

"You have no fucking right," Dan barked back. "You're at my partner's house, yelling through the door at 11pm to try and get me to lie on national TV. You want me to cover for you? You're on another planet. And I can tell you're drunk."

Devon growled. "Knew you wouldn't have the balls to fight me, faggot."

"Oh – there it is," Dan said. He knew it was stupid of him, but he could feel his blood temperature rising; it was a cheap shot, but it was working. He didn't want anybody to think of him as a coward, even somebody like Devon, who didn't matter. "Nice. You're just proving my point right there. You're a homophobic shithead just trying to drag me because you're a bigot. Lucky for you that you started fucking Sarah and stumbled into this; how else would you find an outlet for all that hate?"

"Fuck you," Devon called back – but Dan had had enough. Jeremy finally joined him in the hallway; a robe wrapped around him, and took Dan's arm in his.

"What's he saying?"

"You can guess," Dan said, keeping his voice low so that Devon couldn't hear him through the door. "All the same shit as before – just calling me a faggot now, telling me I'm not brave enough to fight him."

Jeremy sighed, rubbing his arm. "I'm almost sorry to have to restrain you."

"It's alright," said Dan, grinning sideways at him. Jeremy was so tuned into him; it was a comfort to know that Jeremy at least identified with his desire to put this asshole in his place, which they had come to the same conclusion about why that couldn't happen. "I'm sure it'll be satisfying enough to see the downfall of his career."

"I wonder if Sarah knows he's here." Jeremy mused, eyes still fixed on the door. They could hear Devon's banging through it. "We release that CCTV tomorrow and she's got a whole other situation on her hands. I doubt she's going to like that very much."

Dan shrugged. "I guess they both have poor taste in partners."

"They sure do. I'm kind of glad, though."

Dan turned, not following Jeremy's logic. "Yeah?"

"Well," said Jeremy, nestling up against him a little more. "If she hadn't left you, then we probably wouldn't be here right now. Right? And she probably wouldn't have been moved to actually leave you unless she wanted to move in with him. I don't know. It's all... good things coming out of bad things."

"Yeah, I guess you're right."

It only took a couple more minutes before the police arrived. They could see the red and blue lights through the apartment windows, and moved over to watch as Devon was dragged away, really putting up a fight.

Dan winced. "Yeah. She's really not going to want that footage on the news."

"But... you know," said Jeremy. "I think now, at least, we have something better to give Marcie than a bunch of flowers."

Chapter 21

Jeremy's hand was a little clammy in Dan's as they made their way down the red carpet, flashing bulbs winking at them as they walked. Much like the TV interviews, this was new to him – but at least this seemed to be a pleasant experience for him instead of just a horrifying one. He looked so handsome in his dark brown suit, and Dan couldn't even complain about the way he himself looked when he had stepped out of the apartment today.

More important than any of that, however, was that they were attending these sports awards as a couple – their first engagement out together in public.

As far as Dan knew, their good friends Sarah and Devon were meant to be here too – but so far, they hadn't set eyes on the 'happy' couple. From what Marcie has told them this evening, the cops had detained Devon after he resisted arrest. Would he even be out in time to come here? Even if he was, Dan wasn't sure his pride would survive the attention.

Marcie had really made good use of her 'flowers'. Twitter was overloaded with videos of Devon resisting arrest today.

The Marlins hadn't commented so far, but... well. Surely the outlook wasn't good for him. They certainly hadn't moved to defend him.

"This is insane," Jeremy murmured in his ear, eyes scanning the crowds at the ropes around them. For the most part, they had been very receptive of Dan and Jeremy – even excited to see them. Dan could understand Jeremy's elation. He didn't think he'd ever received this much attention on an ordinary event carpet before. "I don't know how to feel."

"Feel flattered," Dan suggested. "I think they like us."

"Well... most of them do."

Dan followed Jeremy's line of sight, eyes resting on a couple of his teammates. They appeared to have already arrived and were standing outside the building's entrance to smoke. Just as Jeremy was implying, they really didn't look pleased to see the couple there – but frankly, that only fueled Dan's fire. He linked his fingers through Jeremy's, turning to smile wider at him, and lifted his hand to kiss it.

"Don't care," he assured him. "I did once, but I don't anymore."

"Not even your father?"

Dan sighed, still keeping his voice quiet enough that the media couldn't pick it up from nearby. "I haven't heard a word from any family. They must have noticed by now. I figured if they want to talk to me about it, they can; it's not like we're close, to begin with. I'll be in touch with them at normal times. Birthdays, Christmas... we'll see how it goes."

"And if they're not interested?"

Dan shrugged. "I guess I'll have to build a new family."

Jeremy's smile flushed wider, leaning into him as they walked past the displeased teammates and into the building. It was much cooler in there with the AC, even now that the evening had begun to cool down outside and Dan sighed with relief as they were pointed towards their table. He could already see Zack waving them over.

"This is Zack?" Jeremy asked.

"The very same," Dan confirmed. "You're going to love him, I'm sure."

And of course, he was right. Zack's hyper humor gelled excellently with Jeremy's warmth. Had it not been for the arrival of Sarah into the room, the evening probably would have continued on nicely unhindered. As she walked in, however, there really was a distinct chill – a couple of whispers from other tables.

"Easy, now," said Zack. "Don't even look at her."

That was easier said than done. Dan hadn't seen Sarah since their argument in the cafe, and could still barely believe that she had made such a concerted effort to lie and ruin his life. The bitterness was completely astounding. After all, she really had no reason to come for him – unless, he supposed, she was trying to set herself up for an easy way to skin his bank account when their divorce inevitably happened. Whatever the reason, it had clearly failed, and now he was surprised that she had even chosen to show her face, especially as Devon did not appear to be with her.

Dan wouldn't have wanted to turn up to this even on his own if Jeremy was indisposed – and the media was actually on his side now. The woman had the nerve; he had to give her that.

Then again, he'd always known that about her. It was one of the things he had loved, once.

She ignored the whispering and took a seat a few tables away, head held high. She was still beautiful, but her appearance was tainted now by the knowledge of what she had done to him – to a man she claimed to have loved. By the sounds of things, Devon felt she had some right to take revenge on Dan. He still wasn't sure why she thought that. Things hadn't been unpleasant between them, just distant.

"You okay?" Jeremy asked his hand on Dan's.

"I'm fine," he promised. "Just thinking."

"There's a first time for everything," teased Zack, bringing the mood back up as Dan leaned across to swat at him. With his friend's distraction helping him, the event seemed to start soon afterward.

Award ceremonies had never been Dan's favorite. He did believe in rewarding excellence in sports, but there were other ways of doing that – winning tournaments, for example, and the Olympics. It wasn't that the people who received the awards didn't deserve them. He just often felt that the announcers and the voters were insincere, rewarding people because they thought it would make themselves look good rather than make the awardee happy.

Today, however, his mind was about to be changed.

He spent most of the ceremony playing with Jeremy's hand, distracted from the events and only applauding when he was supposed to. As such, when Zack pointed at the stage to draw his attention, he had no idea why.

"Next up is the Pioneer Award," said the announcer. Dan wasn't sure what Zack was getting at, as his friend refused to speak – just gestured towards the speaker, indicating that he should listen.

Frankly, it made him a little nervous.

"This award commends excellence in driving the industry forward, either through innovation, charitable outreach, or a variety of different ways. Anybody who advances us as a sporting community forward is eligible. We had many nominations this year, and the following were commended for final consideration."

She reeled off a list of names that Dan recognized – all people who he really admired – but he still couldn't see why Zack was imploring him to pay attention. Only when he recognized the sound of his own name did he begin to understand, and felt stupid. Color flooded into his face as he shot Zack a warning look, but even just his name being spoken into the room was met with riotous applause.

Dan looked around, seeing that neither Sarah nor his homophobic teammates were clapping, but a wide range of other people were. He could see his coach at another table and his PR team; he could see Marcie, who they had managed to score a ticket for. A whole host of other people was on their feet, grins broad and wide.

He couldn't believe this. It felt like a dream. By his side, Jeremy grinned and squeezed his hand.

"You deserve this," he mouthed. Dan didn't feel as though he did – but clearly, the room disagreed. They knew who had won even before the announcer's broad smiling face actually spoke his name. When she did, however, the roars rose around him, and Zack pushed him up onto his feet to send him walking, numbly, towards the stage.

"A late nominee. For his stalwart calmness in the face of homophobic interrogation, concise and inspiring statements of pride, and the bravery to step out of the closet into a distinctly unreceptive environment, the council commends Daniel Carter."

As he reached the stage and the microphone, he knew from the chants of the crowd in the room around him that this celebration was not insincere. Perhaps it often was – but right in this moment, the people who were clapping and cheering undoubtedly really meant it.

He cleared his throat, hovering over the mic for a second as he tried to work out what to say. Then, all at once, it came to him.

"Thank you so much for your support," he said, stumbling over specific words as he dealt with the loud emotions flooding through him. "In this moment and over the past week or so, I've never been tested so hard in my life, and I've never felt such a wall of people behind me. Thank you."

When the noise died down, he pressed on to continue.

"I don't really deserve any of this. I'm not doing anything brave – or at least, I shouldn't be. It shouldn't be a big deal like this to be who you are in front of the world. I'm no saint. The allegations that have been made against me are not true, but the way I treated my partner, Jeremy, at college; I... I suffered from the same internalized homophobia that I feel many young people do. I let it crush me, and crush us, and... I remain sorry for that."

He could make out Jeremy's face in the crowd, open and brimming with affection.

"I know not everybody in this room supports me. I respect that. Honestly, I understand it. Like I just said, I don't feel I deserve this award just for being who I am – but I will accept it on the basis that now is the time we move forward as a community. It should not be an event when a person comes out. It should not be front page news. I hope that anybody listening to me now with disgust or dislike can look at me and know that I tolerate you, just as you are capable of tolerating me. Really, that's all I ask. And to anybody who has lied about me…"

The sound in the room dipped, straining to hear whatever insult he delivered in Sarah's direction now – but as he looked at her, and even before he did, he knew that wasn't the route he would take. She was alone, after all, and Dan had never been like her. Not for one moment.

"I'm sorry you felt the need to do that. I hope that in the future, you come to a place in your life that doesn't require you to hurt other people to proceed or prevail. When you do, the rest of us will be waiting. That's the reason I accept this award. That's what progress and forgiveness and unity are all about, and that is what I stand for tonight, and going forward. Thank you so much."

As he stepped away from the stage, an award in hand, all he wanted to do was to dive into Jeremy's arms and hide his face – but despite the embarrassment of having an entire room of people roar with approval, he couldn't help but feel lifted by it too. Maybe Jeremy was right. Maybe this award and everything that followed from it would be their opportunity to change the world, and to make it better for people who existed in his position.

"You did so well up there," said Jeremy, his voice a little choked up as he tugged Dan close to him, peppering kisses over his cheek. "God, it was like – just like looking at you back in college, Dan. The old you, the you that didn't even know how to be scared."

"We like him," said Zack, ruffling up his hair and beaming with pride. "We want more of fearless Dan. He's going to win us the season. He's going to change the landscape of the sport. Tolerance, man. We're going to get there."

"More fearless Dan," he promised, leaning back to look Jeremy directly in the eyes. "I swear, from now on." Dan didn't need to tell Jeremy that he loved him; he could feel it pouring directly between them purely through the eye contact, and it completely eliminated the need to communicate aloud. Jeremy gripped his hand hard and refused to let go.

No matter how hard their world had been rocked at college, and no matter how far down Dan had buried his true self for all those years following it, they had finally come through and won. When they went home tonight and made love, it would be absent of the fear they had been feeling for the past few days and the residual overarching fear that the sports world they lived in didn't want them.

Clearly, by the sounds of this crowd, the world of sports absolutely did.

Part of him wanted to go and reconcile with Sarah, to support her in this time when he imagined the people around her were being pretty cold towards her. After all, they had been married for several years, and though he had been withdrawn from her, he had not been without fondness or affection for her. It was hard for him to let go completely of feeling protective – but as he glanced over at her with the invitation in his eyes, he saw only hatred in hers.

Well, he thought. I didn't burn that bridge. And he hadn't, nor had he burned it with Devon, whether the man was still with the cops or simply too ashamed to come here tonight. All he had done was to exist as his authentic, honest self. If they wanted to continue trying to criticize him for that, well... they could go right ahead. Even now he knew the full extent of how manipulative Sarah was comfortable being, he wasn't afraid of her anymore. He had walked through fire and survived.

In fact, he hadn't just survived. He had come back happier and stronger.

The world was his oyster. He had no secrets left – and with Jeremy by his side, he didn't plan to write any new ones into his future.

Epilogue

It was the height of the hockey season, and he had been forced to rush straight out of training with Zack and the others to make it here – but regardless, Dan still made time to attend Jeremy's high school games. They were important to his partner, so they had to be equally important to him. Besides, his presence at these games seemed to encourage sponsors to donate more money to the team. That money went directly to helping the players get hockey scholarships, and for managing their expenses in college – and if that rescued just one kid from having to rely on his parents for money, then Dan would have done his job.

In fact, Dan had already done his job. As he watched the players mill about now at half-time, he caught sight of one of the players he recognized grinning at him and waving – and he grinned and waved back. This was Robbie, who had been absolutely thrilled to approach Dan after a game a few months ago. Dan could still remember every word.

"Oh man," he'd opened with, offering his hand for Dan to shake – and then refusing to let go. "Dude, you have no idea how excited I am to meet you. I'm a huge fan."

"It's great to meet you too," Dan had said, a little taken aback. Usually, his fans were polite and excited, but this was a lot more than he was used to.

"I mean, obviously, you're coach's boyfriend, so that's one thing, and I think you're an incredible player, but... your interview with GQ, man? That fucking changed my life."

"Language, Robbie," his mother had said, standing a few feet away – but she was smiling.

"Sorry, mom." The kid had grinned, turning back to his idol. "I'm serious, man. Before you came out, I thought I'd never make it in professional hockey. Like... I thought I'd have to hide a huge part of myself, you know? I'd have to give up on my dream or my freedom, and you showed me I could have both, so..."

He had even looked a little choked up, and the whole thing had seriously moved Dan. Robbie didn't look choked up now as he waved from the pitch – but nor would Dan want him to. His braveness with coming out had changed that kid's life, and that made his head spin.

Of course, that wasn't the best thing about his life – and as he looked around to find Jeremy, he finally set eyes on him and the platinum engagement band on his finger as he saluted from the sidelines. Dan saluted back, fully aware of how lucky he was. His family wouldn't talk to him anymore, and on occasion, he still got shitty comments on social media from people who, for some reason, continued to believe Sarah, but that was okay. He was forming a new family here, a family that loved him for every single part of him, not just the traditionally acceptable parts.

Wasn't that what everybody wanted, in the end?

*****

Don't miss out!

Visit the website below and you can sign up to receive emails whenever Van Cole publishes a new book. There's no charge and no obligation.

https://books2read.com/r/B-A-RTRV-MLZDC

Also by Van Cole

3 Man Huddle: MMM Best Friend Romance
His Alpha Wolf: Gay First Time Romance
A Dragon's Miracle: Gay Dragon MPREG Romance
Double-Teamed: MMM First Time Football Romance
His Football Star: Gay Second Chance Romance
Love In My Town: MM First Time Romance
Training A Hockey Star
Game Night
Double Shift
Take A Shot
Dear Professor
Getting Inked
Ninth Inning
Triple Threat
Seducing My Best Friend's Brother
My Protector
The Blueprint
Show Me The Way
End Zone
Matched To His Tiger
Love At First Puck
My Straight Boss
Falling For The Alpha
My Boss
On Thin Ice